HALF MY FACEBOOK FRIENDS ARE FERRETS

J. A. Buckle

Curious Fox

First published in 2014 by Curious Fox, an imprint of Capstone
Global Library Limited, 7 Pilgrim Street, London, EC4V 6LB –
Registered company number: 6695582

www.curious-fox.com

Text © J. A. Buckle 2014

The author's moral rights are hereby asserted.

ISBN 978 1 782 02074 5
17 16 15 14 13
10 9 8 7 6 5 4 3 2 1

A CIP catalogue for this book is available from the British Library.

Printed and bound by CPI Group (UK) Ltd, Croydon, CR0 4YY
Typeset in Weiss 11 pt

To Sophie and Jasmine,
for being inspirational

Monday 6th January – 6 months till my 16th birthday

10.20am: Lower Dungeon (AKA English Block)

Today I have to do a presentation at school. It counts towards my English GCSE, so I feel I should make an effort. Mrs Barber, our English teacher, refuses to let on just how much it counts, which makes me a bit suspicious. I wouldn't be surprised if it's less than half a percent.

At least my presentation should be interesting. So far, we've had to sit through "Nail art through the ages", "Cheryl Cole – Style Queen" and "Eating for a healthy complexion". I'm still wondering if I've made the right choice though. I had three ideas originally:

Ferrets, their role in modern society

The Major Pentatonic Scale and its use in improvising riffs

The satanic roots of Death Metal

I decided to go with the last one, feeling it had the edge excitement-wise, but now I wonder if it might be a bit too exciting, especially for Mrs Barber who's nearing retirement and rumoured to have heart trouble.

"Who do we have next?" says Mrs Barber, consulting her list. "Ah yes, Joshua. Come on up, dear."

Mrs Barber beckons me to the front and I suddenly notice the St Christopher hanging round her neck. My PowerPoint has pictures of church burnings!

To calm my nerves I take a few deep breaths and remember Ollie's advice of imagining everyone in the room naked. Unfortunately, Charlotte Anderson is in the front row and imagining her naked sets off a stirring below. This would be fine if my trousers weren't so tight but Mum refuses to buy new ones due to our Financial Difficulties.

"Do you have a PowerPoint?" Mrs Barber asks.

"Pardon! Oh yes, um. Yes, I do," I admit.

"Excellent," she says. "Some nice slides for us to look at."

"Right… sort of… not really."

Mrs Barber looks a bit uncertain. "What exactly is your presentation on, dear?"

3.50pm: halfway down some road or other

"Fantastic presentation," says Ollie on the way home. "Especially that bit where you showed the slide of the demon with three willies and Mrs Barber had the panic attack."

"Thank you, Ollie," I say. "Damn! I knew I should've done the one on ferrets."

"I shouldn't worry," Ollie goes on. "Mrs Barber will be OK; a short stay in hospital will probably do her good."

I say goodbye to Ollie at the corner of his road and wander on home. Thankfully, no one is in to ask how the nightmare presentation went. In my bedroom, I say hi to Ozzy, my ferret, and reach under the bed for the giant leather-bound notebook Mum gave me. Yeah, I know – some people get PlayStations for Christmas, I get a notebook.

At the time, Mum tried to "big up" the present by saying, "It's got 200 pages of extra high-quality paper!"

"Amazing," I said.

"So, you can write on both sides without the ink showing through."

"Awesome Mum, really awesome."

"But the important thing," she droned on, "is that this can be your release valve, Josh. When I was young, I wrote down all the bad things that happened to me in a book like this and I felt much better. It got out all the angry, destructive feelings."

Maybe you should write one again then, I thought, but I just nodded and laid the book with my other gifts (a festive white Toblerone and a packet of scented gel pens).

Now, I'm wondering if I should use it for its original purpose. I need a bit of a release valve one way or another. I open the book and make a list of things that are bad in my life. It's not complete – that would take hours – but it's a start:

9

Things that are bad in my life:

1. I am 15½ and have never been kissed, unless you count my nan, Mum, Mrs Stokes, Aunt Sarah, Ollie's Labrador Bongo and my cousin Anna. And Bongo's kiss was more of a slurp.

2. I look nerdy and I don't even wear glasses

3. We have Financial Difficulties

4. My mother is the strictest parent on the planet

5. Girls think I'm a dick...

Good. Excellent. Do I feel any better?
No.

Tuesday 7th January

1.10pm: astroturf with Peter, Davey and Ollie

"Looking at me," I say, "would you say I come across a bit nerdy?"

"Nah," says Ollie. "You're too stupid to be nerdy."

"Thanks," I say. "But I mean, if you didn't know that?"

"I'd put you down more as a geek," says Davey.

"A geek! Davey, if anyone is a geek it's you."

"Er, I may be a lot of things but I am not a geek."

"You are a bit," I say.

"Just because I wear glasses…"

"What about your periodic table mug?" I remind him.

"That was a gift."

"The University Challenge quiz books?"

"I was going through a phase."

"The Apollo 13 space module poster on your door?"

Davey holds up his hands. "OK, you got me."

"Anyway," says Ollie, "I don't think being nerdy's so bad. I saw a girl once with a sweatshirt that said 'I love nerds' on it. At least, I think that's what it said. It wasn't easy to make out because of her enormous boobs."

"Right," I say.

"The words were kinda stretched."

"Yes Ollie, we get it."

"Well, all I know," says Peter, "is that whatever you are, you should be proud."

"Jesus, Peter," Ollie says, "that is so gay."

"I know," says Peter happily.

Wednesday 8th January

4.45pm: Inner Sanctum (AKA bedroom)

School seemed to go on forever today but when I check my bag I discover it's still not over because I now have a mountain of maths to finish! Mr Cain, our teacher, obviously thinks none of us have anything better to do than slave over decimals all evening. In my case, he may be right, but he's not to know that.

5.20pm

The phone rings and I rush downstairs. It's Davey. Why he can't text like normal kids is beyond me.

"Have you done your maths?" he says.

"A bit," I say.

"I don't get it."

"What don't you get?"

"Anything!"

Davey sounds desperate but I'm used to this. He knows how to turn on the emotional blackmail and while it works with his mum, it won't work with me.

"Well, maybe you should ask Mr Cain," I say.

"Huh?"

"Mr Cain, our maths teacher."

"But then he'll realise I'm dumb and move me down. And I won't survive ten minutes with the chavs, Josh!"

I can hear Davey's breathing down the phone, short and rapid, like he's just climbed Mount Everest, or in Davey's case, walked down his hallway.

"Calm down, Davey," I say. "Let's go through it slowly. Now what you need to do…"

"Can't you just tell me the answers?"

"What?"

"Hollyoaks is on."

5.30pm: back in Inner Sanctum

I'm a soft touch, that's the trouble. Even Ozzy takes advantage of my wonderful nature. Currently he is rolling around in my school uniform scattering an asthmatic's nightmare of black and white hairs. I'm getting the occasional whiff of ferret food too. Thanks Ozzy. I'm really gonna attract the opposite sex with my trousers smelling of liver!

Thursday 9th January

3.15pm: La Bastille (AKA French)

Madam Zizi, our French teacher, has just told us to write a paragraph on our family but as I don't know the French for "ridiculously bad-tempered psychos", it's gonna be difficult. Madam Zizi says we can finish our paragraph at home.

Does one sentence count as a paragraph?

Absolutely it does, which means I can spend the entire evening chilling out to Megadeth and designing a cool CD sleeve for my album. Yes!!

Looking at me, you would never guess I'm a metal head. I look more into Abba or the Cardiff over-80s male voice choir, than I do into Morbid Angel or Slayer. This is because my mum insists that my hair is kept short and in the least fashionable style known to man. She also believes that wearing black T-shirts is satanic. My mother is the most repressed, nun-like person I know. How she ever had kids is beyond me.

6.00pm: kitchen

Currently Mother Superior is out tending to the needs of the various folks she looks after, so I make myself a delicious tea of cornflakes and smoky bacon crisps.

I have only just finished and am debating whether it's bad to eat four bowls of cornflakes in a row when Mum and my sister come in. My sister kicks off her stilettos and collapses in the chair opposite. She looks like she's had a fight with a hair drier but I don't want to die a virgin, so I decide not to mention this.

"Good day at work, Maddie?" I say.

"F * * * off," she replies.

I have an on/off relationship with my sister.

Mostly off.

Mum is shifting things round in the fridge. "Don't tell me someone's used up all the milk," she mutters.

"Not me," I say, moving my maths folder in front of my cereal bowl.

"Mrs Hughes down the road has a fridge that warns you when the milk is low," says Maddie.

"Does she now," says Mum.

"She got it as part of that ten grand refit she had on her kitchen."

I give Mum a sympathetic look but she has turned to fill up the kettle.

Sadly, it'd take ten grand to bring our house up to squatter's standards. Not that it's dirty or anything, it's just caught in a 70s time warp. We could make money by opening it as a museum. "And here you see genuine 1970s wallpaper. Note the globular pattern in shades of burnt umber. Sick bags can be found to your right."

Also, a lot of things don't work. I've given up eating fish fingers due to the three foot drifts of snow in our freezer, and the last time I tried using the oven, I was almost incinerated.

Mum says this is what happens when you don't have a man about the place. Which is a bit hurtful considering I'm nearly 16 and definitely of the male persuasion, but I know what she means. We don't have Dad is what she means.

Saturday 11th January

10.45am: Inner Sanctum

Today is an Ozzy cleaning day. As I get out his towel and the ferret shampoo, Ozzy eyes me suspiciously through his black bandit mask. He does not like being washed.

11.10am

Hmm, the bathroom looks like it's been hit by a tsunami. My clothes are soaking wet. I have several large scratches on the inside of my arms and a bruise coming where I smacked my head on the sink.

Ozzy is very clean though!

He is also very annoyed.

Sunday 12th January

3.30pm: Mr Pitman's house

I am young, not suffering with any serious health issues and am a "drain on resources", which in Mum's eyes means I should be working. Never mind that I have homework, and must wash Ozzy, and update my Facebook account and spy on other people's accounts to find out what amazing stuff they're up to so that I can feel really jealous. This is not enough for my mum; she'd have me digging turnips in the snow at 5am if she had her way. In fact, she has me doing something worse – entertaining Mr Pitman.

Mr Pitman lives down the road from us and suffers with

arthritis. When it's bad, he can hardly bend to put on his socks. Ever since his wife left last year, Mum has been cleaning and shopping for him. And since Mum is great at guilt-tripping me into doing anything she wants, I walk his dog (a yappy Yorkshire terrier). I also mow his lawn and play chess or, on very depressing days, Ludo. Mr Pitman always wins because, try as I might, I cannot get into a game of Ludo.

Maybe if it was strip Ludo with Megan Fox... Anyway, where was I? Oh yes, moving my little green counter.

Mr Pitman throws the dice with vigour, causing it to spring off the board and land in Minty's basket (Minty is the dog).

"Whoops, sorry," says Mr Pitman as I delve into Minty's hair encrusted blankets.

"Grrr," says Minty.

"She won't hurt you," says Mr Pitman. "She's only a little thing."

Yes, but her teeth are like hypodermic needles I feel like saying, but Minty has remembered that I'm her ticket out of this hell-hole so she resists savaging my face.

"Your go," says Mr Pitman.

It's the weekend and I should be getting up to all sorts of teenage shenanigans. Instead I'm sat here feeling my brain about to implode through lack of use. I roll a two.

"Unlucky," says Mr Pitman.

Monday 13th January

9.35am: Tower of Terror (AKA Maths Block)

Mr Pitman's house is depressing but it has nothing on school. If one more person says to me: "Cheer up lad, these are the best days of your life!" I may have to pin them down, attach electrodes to their private parts and send several thousand volts of electricity coursing through their bodies. These are certainly NOT the best days of my life. At least, I bloody well hope not!

Today in Maths, for example, Mr Cain informs me that he's had to give me an F for my homework because the writing was so bad "You are 15, Joshua," he says. "You should be able to write."

I say, you are 50, Mr Cain; you should be able to read!

Actually, I just nod and promise to write it out again.

10.45am: Field of Nightmares (AKA school playing fields)

And now in PE, Lydia Smart has just come over and said to me, "There's a party at Hannah Harrigan's on Saturday. Don't bother coming, you're not invited."

What was the point in that? She just walked right round the pitch to tell me that.

There are girls in this school who are downright nasty. They make Simon Cowell look like Ghandi. Not that I'd want to go to Hannah Harrigan's party. Her dad is something big in the Metropolitan Police. He'd probably arrest you for dropping a crisp.

Davey comes and stands beside me and we watch the two teams slog up one end of the field, miss the goal and slog back down again. No one seems very enthusiastic apart from Mr Cox, the PE teacher. People must be able to hear him shouting in France.

Davey wipes his nose on the bottom of his PE shirt and says, "Did Hannah ask you to her party?"

"No," I say. "She asked me not to it, or rather her brainless buddy Lydia did."

"Me too," says Davey.

I look at Davey shivering in his XXL T-shirt. "Cheer up," I say. "Girls' parties are lame anyway."

"How do you know?"

"Well, I don't know for sure. But they have to be. I mean all they do is giggle and give each other manicures."

"Yes, but there'll be boys there," says Davey. "Most of the boys in our class are going."

"Really?" I say.

Mr Cox is beckoning us onto the pitch. "Shift them lazy arses!" he yells. If you closed your eyes, you could imagine you were on drill in Iraq. Accept for the rain, mud and extreme cold, that is.

I notice Lydia has been chosen to bully off, which is pretty appropriate. I am determined to whack her hard in the ankles at least twice before the match is over. I may even aim higher.

Most of the boys in the class. What a cow.

5.45pm: Inner Sanctum

I am late home because I've had to stay and brush leaves off the Astroturf. I am definitely off Mr Cox's Christmas list. He has a bruise the size of Jupiter on his shin but how was I to know he'd dive in the way just as I was about to clobber Lydia. It's his fault for being so enthusiastic.

Tuesday 14th January

5.00pm: Inner Sanctum, writing in my leather-bound notebook

Got no respect for Lydia Smart

Girls like her can't touch my heart

If I had to choose between her or death

I'd dig my grave and hold my breath

From the album: *No respect for Lydia* Smart by Joshua Walker

Right, so I'm rubbish at looking cool, attracting women and getting invited places. On the bright side though, I'm awesome on guitar!

The only problem is that due to Financial Difficulties I can't have a Randy Rhoads Flying V Jackson with blue ghost flames, ebony fingerboard and mother-of-pearl shark fin inlays (£499.95, Steve's Music Emporium in town). In fact, I can't have an electric guitar at all. Mr Trumper, the music teacher at school, reckons my acoustic will give me an excellent start, but what he doesn't realise is that my acoustic is a child's, three-quarter size, nylon string classical. It's great for "Greensleaves", crap for "Highway to Hell".

Anyway, I play a bit of the classical masterpiece "Spanish Romance", which I can do pretty well and am just about to consult my Vladimir Axegrinder, *Death Metal for Dummies* book, when Ozzy scampers over and starts jumping about and gnawing the cover. Ozzy has no respect: Vladimir is an icon of death metal guitar tuition.

The doorbell rings and I go downstairs. Davey's standing in the porch looking red. Combined with his short hair and round face he looks like a worried beetroot.

"I hate girls," he says.

I nod, thinking that maybe Lydia or Hannah has made some cruel remark about his huge nose, festering spots or terrible hairstyle.

Davey prods me in the chest. "Aren't you gonna ask me in?" he says.

"Sorry," I say. "Come up."

Upstairs Davey collapses heavily on my bed, which is worrying because if the legs break I'll be sleeping on the floor for the next ten years.

"I wish I was twelve," he says.

I raise my eyebrows.

"I hate being a teenager."

"Ah..."

"I hate having these... you know... urges..."

I know where Davey's coming from here. One of the worst things about being a teenager is that girls (some of them at least) start to look attractive. I preferred it when they were annoying little wannabe princesses running round with ice cream down their fronts and Barbie dolls in their knickers. (This refers to my cousin Anna who is seriously weird and probably not representative of most little girls.)

"Mum will never speak to me again," Davey goes on.

"What's happened, Davey?"

"She will never forgive me…"

"Davey! What's happened?"

What had happened was that Davey had decided to deal with his urges by taking matters into his own hands… literally! He had laid on his bed, closed his eyes, put some music on his headphones and… well… got busy.

Anyway, a short time later he thought, Hey, what I fancy now is a nice hot drink. He opened his eyes and there on the table beside his bed was a steaming hot mug of tea!

"Are you sure it wasn't there before?" I ask him. "Maybe you forgot you made it."

"I didn't forget."

"Your mind was on other things," I remind him.

"Josh, either I have developed amazing telepathic powers or… my mum brought it in a few minutes earlier."

"Oh," I say. "Eeew!"

"Thanks!"

I sympathise with Davey but at least his mum understands about men and their urges. My mum understands nothing. If she burst in on me doing that, she'd send me off to some Tibetan monastery to get castrated or beheaded or something.

If Dad was around it would be easier but Dad will never be around. My dad died when I was a baby. He worked on the

North Sea oilrigs as a driller. Strangely, he didn't die in some horrific drilling accident but through a plain old heart attack. Turns out he had a congenital heart defect that no one knew about. Luckily, me and my sister don't have it, or so Mum says. Anyway, Dad was only 31 when he died so he will always look young, cool and super-strong, like he does in his photo on the cabinet in the hall.

I send Davey on his way with the thought that it could've been worse. It could have been his nan come in with the tea. She might have thought he was having a seizure and called for an ambulance. I think that made Davey feel better.

Wednesday 15th January

10.10pm: Inner Sanctum

I take out the leather-bound notebook and rip out the page about things that are bad in my life. Who needs that kind of negativity? Instead, in the same way people write lists of places they should see before they die I am writing a list of things I should do before I'm 16. Currently they are:

1. Be kissed by someone who is female but not a relative, very old, very young or covered in fur. i.e. get a girlfriend!

2. Master the legendary "One" by Metallica.

3. See Children of Bodom live – I may have to travel to Finland for this, but that is a small

price to pay, at least metaphorically.

4. Be the proud owner of the Randy Rhodes Flying V Jackson with blue ghost flames, ebony fingerboard and mother-of-pearl shark fin inlays.

5. Get something pierced or tattooed!

6. Be half as cool as people say my dad was.

The easiest (or least impossible) of these is probably number 2, so I go and print out the tab for "One" from the computer. It is over nine pages long! Luckily, I am not 16 for another five and a half months.

Friday 17th January

8.15pm: Transept to Forbidding Portal (AKA hallway)

Brill, a letter for me! I hardly ever get letters.

I rip open the envelope and find that I have qualified for a "50 percent reduction" on the cost of a Stanna stairlift.

WTF?

Saturday 18th January

1.10pm: kitchen

I am sitting eating my lunch (family bag of smoky bacon crisps) and enjoying a fantastic metal-stardom daydream where I am being suffocated by hordes of adoring, insanely attractive female fans, when who should come in but my sister and her crappy boyfriend, Clint.

I mean "Clint" – what sort of a name is that? It sounds more like a furniture polish than a person.

"Whatcha dude," says Clint, giving me a hard thump on the back. "Got yourself a girlfriend yet?"

"Don't tease him," says my sister, switching on the kettle.

"I ain't teasing; good-lookin' guy like him should be fighting 'em off with a stick."

"I don't have time for a girlfriend," I tell him. "I'm concentrating on my exams." Unlike some idiots I could mention who wouldn't know a GCSE if it came up and bit him on the goolies.

"Yeah right," says Clint. "Lot of good that'll do yer. Look at me, not one GC thingy to me name and I did alright."

"You're unemployed," I remind him.

Clint leans over and slams both fists on the table. He really is massive; his arms are wider than most people's bodies.

"That's cause there's no jobs!" he roars. "You think I wanna be outta work!"

"Clint hon, leave him alone," says my sister. "He didn't mean it."

"Yes, well, I'm going on Facebook," I say, getting up from the table.

"Oh yeah," Clint laughs. "Bet you got loadsa friends, eh?"

"Quite a few," I say.

"Shame most of 'em are ferrets!"

Even my traitor of a sister laughs at this.

I leave the room without replying. How dare he? Less than half my Facebook friends are ferrets.

Monday 20th January

5.50pm: kitchen (Mother Superior not yet home)

My sister bought me a small bottle of Heineken today, probably as a peace offering. I hide it behind my wardrobe out of Mum's way. Mum says alcohol causes nothing but pain and torment but God knows why she thinks that; my life is full of pain and torment and I've hardly had any.

Anyway, if Maddie thinks she can buy my forgiveness with beer she's… probably right.

Tuesday 21st January

8.00pm: Inner Sanctum

I've decided that in order to be cool like my dad (number 6 on my list) I need to build up some muscles. Needless to say, we don't have any proper weight-training equipment so I have to use whatever comes to hand. In this case, a large bottle of Coke (three-quarters drunk) and Ozzy. At first Ozzy likes being lifted up and down. He makes excited dooking noises and looks interestedly at all the cobwebs on the walls, but then he gets scared and lets out a fart. An eye-wateringly bad one! Jeez, I bet Dad didn't have to put up with farting ferrets when he was weight-training.

Wednesday 22nd January

11.00pm: Inner Sanctum, listening to Children of Bodom on my headphones

I wonder how much it costs to go to Finland...

Thursday 23rd January

6.30pm: kitchen with Mother Superior

"Finland!" announces my mum. "Listen to me, Josh, if I can ever afford to go abroad on holiday, which seems unlikely given our Financial Difficulties then I certainly won't be going to some God-forsaken place where it snows nine tenths of the year and barely sees daylight. I will go to Corfu."

I feel I should point out the huge geographical and meteorological inaccuracies in this statement but I can't be bothered. My mother has no soul. It's no good telling her that Finland is the coolest place on the planet. That there are 2,500 metal bands there, which in a country with a population of 5 million, means that every 200th person is in a band. I mean, if you had to come up with a similar statistic for where I live, it'd probably be every 200th person has a Zimmer frame!

"Finland," says my mum again. She has the nerve to pat me on the head and chuckle as I open the front door.

I say, for f***'s sake Mum, you are about as adventurous as an egg and cress sandwich!

Actually, I say: "Bye then. Peter's mum is bringing me home."

7.00pm: Scouts

People think Scouts is for little kids but I go to Explorer Scouts, which is for 14–16 year olds. True, it's not an activity you'd usually associate with metal, but a few girls go and there's always a chance one of them might help me out with my sheep-shanks!

Tonight we are doing trust exercises. These have the potential for bodily contact but suddenly I notice that none of the girls are here. Great! Now, I'm facing bodily contact with a load of sweaty, spot-infested boys. I may as well touch myself up.

In the first activity, we have to form a circle while a blindfolded Explorer stands in the centre, arms folded over his chest. The "victim" then leans forward and is caught by one of us and pushed back to the middle. One thing's for sure, I definitely don't want to go in the centre. Not because I'm scared but because I'm 5 foot 11 and so about 3 foot taller than everyone else. When they see me looming towards them they'll scatter like dropped peas! Shaun our leader will realise this though and pick one of the smaller ones.

"Josh, in the centre please."

"But..."

The hall is suddenly full of chicken impersonators so I am forced to accept my fate. My nose is just about my only decent feature but soon it'll be a busted-up wreck.

"Good luck," says a husky female voice.

I turn and come face-to-face with the most beautiful girl I've ever seen. Well, maybe not the most beautiful. I mean there are better-looking people in films and maybe even in Morrisons, but she is pretty good. Also, she seems to be a bit of a rock chick. I am just trying to work out if the thing on her nose is a stud or a bogey when Shaun yanks the blindfold down over my head and propels me into the centre.

5 minutes later

Well, the last five minutes were some of the scariest of my life. My nose remained intact but my bladder nearly didn't and I'm feeling pretty relieved when I remove the blindfold and take my place back in the circle.

"Hmm," says Shaun. "You were a bit rough with Joshua. Sure he's a big lad and can take it, but I want things to be a lot less manic this time."

Thanks, Shaun, nice of you to show your concern.

"Now as some of you may have noticed, we have a new recruit tonight," Shaun goes on. "Would you like to go in the centre, Charlene?"

Charlene has got a nose stud. And a Pantera tattoo. I can't believe it. A girl into metal and I am just about to catch her in my arms!

Very gently, Charlene is moved around the circle. Some of the boys look panic-stricken as she leans their way but, typically, she is not pushed towards me once. Oh well, it looks like we are moving onto something else now.

"Right, as you see, we have some benches and buckets laid out," says Shaun, waving around the hall. "I want you to choose a partner and lead them blindfold around the course."

I feel dreadful; my friend Peter who I knew before I was born (his mum and mine were at antenatal classes together) starts making his way over, but Charlene has already come and stood beside me! In the corner of my eye, I can see Peter's rejected look. Now he will have to be paired with someone by Shaun, or worse still, go with Shaun himself. The embarrassment will be crushing. Still, it can't be helped...

"So you're Josh," Charlene says.

"Certainly am," I say. "Yep, that's me alright... Er, I can't help noticing you're into metal," I go on quickly.

"Defo," she says, giving me the metal salute. "I've seen loadsa bands."

"Awesome," I say.

"Slayer, Metallica, Napalm Death. And I've been to Tuska."

"Tuska?"

"You know, the famous Finnish metal festival."

"Oh, that Tuska," I say.

Charlene puts on her blindfold and grabs my arm. "You should go with your mates."

"Yeah, totally," I say. I don't tell her that Davey is into modern jazz; Ollie, R&B; and Peter, Susan Boyle.

While we're navigating the benches I ruffle my scarf a little and untuck my shirt to try and hide the fact that my Explorer trousers go up to my armpits.

"Josh, what a state you're in today," yells Shaun from the other side of the room. "You won't impress our new girl with your shirt all untucked."

I huff dramatically.

"And what is up with your woggle? Straighten it, please."

Charlene takes off the blindfold and gives me a grin. "He's a bit fussy, isn't he?"

"Yeah," I say. "Fascist pig!"

Luckily, Shaun doesn't hear this or I'd be out of Explorers for good.

9.35pm

"Will you be here next week then?" Shaun asks Charlene as she puts on her coat.

"I'm not sure," she says. I think I may be dying my hair."

9.40pm

"Well, nice girl but somehow I don't think it was her thing," says Shaun when Charlene has gone and it's just me and Peter waiting to get picked up.

"It was Josh's fault," Peter says. "He scared her off with his wonky woggle."

Friday 24th January

7.30pm: front room

I spend about an hour on our crappy, second-hand computer trying to find Charlene on Facebook. You'd think with a name like that it would be easy but the only possible Charlene lives in Bloomsburg, Pennsylvania, which is a bit too far to come for Scouts. I'm starting to wonder if she made up that name to sound cool. Probably her real name is Mavis Block or something. I start typing Mavis Block into Facebook's search box but then realise

I'm being seriously bonkers. Ah well, number 1 on my list will have to wait a bit longer. I must let Charlene go and move on.

Saturday 25th January

2.30pm: lounge

Mum says that one of "her people" (as she calls the folks she makes a living cleaning, cooking and shopping for) knows someone who knows someone who used to work in that pub behind the Co-op called the Dead Duck and that they could get me a job there, maybe. Would I like that?

"Yes," I say. "I'd love to work in a dive called the Dead Duck full of saddo lonely drunks." It's not really called the Dead Duck but it was something like that.

Mum gets annoyed and mentions Financial Difficulties about sixty million times.

I say, "Oh, go on then."

She smiles and leaves. Damn her.

Monday 27th January

7.00pm: Inner Sanctum, doing homework

The trouble with being 15, or one of them, is that there are so many decisions to make. I'm now wondering if I should have taken History rather than Geography:

Rivers or Russians?

Hurricanes or Hitler?

Well, it's too late now.

History sounds dead easy though. At lunch today, Ollie said his teacher told him that World War I started because of a sandwich. Apparently, after this Serbian terrorist failed to assassinate Franz Ferdinand (the Archduke, not the band) he went to a cafe for a quick snack. Then, just as he came out, Franz happened to be there after making a wrong turn in his car. The Serbian grabbed his gun and immediately shot Franz in the neck.

I tried to respond with a similarly interesting story about sedimentary rocks but none came to mind.

Wednesday 29th January

I receive a pair of extra large tan support tights in post.

Why?

Thursday 30th January

7.50pm: Scouts

I give Peter my support tights and am surprised at how offended he gets.

He says, "Just because I'm almost certainly gay doesn't mean I want to dress up in women's tights. Besides, I'm a small."

I notice he doesn't give them back, however.

Saturday 1st February

7.20pm: Inner Sanctum

Ozzy has come to investigate my English literature book, *To Kill a Mockingbird*. Most ferrets probably would kill a mocking bird given half a chance, but Ozzy is about as aggressive as a fondant fancy. A door bangs somewhere and Ozzy jumps and does a little pee on page 10. I feel I should apologise to Harper Lee but she's a multimillionaire, so I don't.

Anyway, it's Saturday evening and I'm stuck inside writing an essay for my English homework. How sad is that? After half an hour I've still only written forty-eight words and twenty of those are the question. Ozzy starts dancing and hopping about on the paper, which isn't helping. I try to nudge him off but he thinks I'm fooling around and runs off with my pen. Can't he tell that I'm not in the mood for games? That I'm slowly dying inside?

Like a mockingbird
Whose song is unheard
Whose beak has been tied
Slowly dying inside

From the album: *Slowly Dying Inside* by Josh Walker

Sunday 2nd February

2.00pm: Inner Sanctum

Crap day today, I have broken a string on my guitar so I can't practise, which is seriously annoying since I still have another eight and three-quarter pages of the "One" Metallica tab to get through.

Monday 3rd February

6.15pm: Inner Sanctum

Another crap day! Mrs Barber said that "My ferret stole my pen", was not a good enough excuse for failing to hand in my *Mockingbird* homework and gave me a detention.

Then, after I got home, Mum had a massive rant at me just for being in her room.

"I don't want you poking around," she said. "I have certain things in there that are... private."

Honestly, all I'd wanted was some of that perfume she keeps for special occasions. Ozzy had a little accident on the carpet and I wanted to cover up the smell. This is what I get for trying to keep things clean and hygienic round here!

Anyway, I've got a French exam tomorrow so I'd better start revising.

Tuesday 4th February – 5 months till my 16th birthday

10.15am: La Bastille (French oral exam)

"When you're ready," says Madame Zizi.

I stutter off the paragraph I have learnt about my hobbies, friends and family. Luckily, the English and French words for guitar are more or less the same, so that's at least one word I've got right.

Throughout my speech Madame Zizi grimaces and pulls at her hair.

Probably not a very good sign.

Thursday 6th February

7.30pm: front room

Scouts is not on tonight as Shaun has injured his thumb demonstrating knots and lashings to the Tuesday Beaver group.

I decide to have a quick look on Facebook in case any ravishing girls have sent me a friend request. A girlfriend request even.

Nope, no friend requests but I do have four "FantasticFarm" requests from Ollie to harvest his crops, rake his leaves, water his onions and build some new stables.

I have three "PurrfectPets" requests from Davey to pamper his puppies, feed the parrot and stroke his rabbits.

And I have two "MasterDinerChef" requests from Peter to mop out the toilets and make two dozen iced American muffins before 9.00pm.

9.45pm

I log out of Facebook feeling exhausted. I may have to delete my account if this goes on.

Friday 7th February

3.00pm: Inner Sanctum

Mum comes in (without knocking) and tells me I have a try-out at The Deceased Duck tomorrow. 'Isn't it exciting?" she says.

"Extremely," I answer.

Mum smiles and leaves. Sarcasm is lost on her.

8.10pm

Hold on, though. If Mum lets me keep my earnings I may actually be able to afford the wondrous Jackson Flying V thereby achieving number 4 on my list. Now that is exciting!

Saturday 8th February

7.00pm: local dive

Yay! I have been taken on as an employee at The Duck Revived. My job isn't very demanding brain-wise but it does mean I have super-clean hands. Yep, I am head washer-upper. Actually, I'm the only washer-upper. Anyway, Mum'll be pleased. From now on she'll probably only mention Financial Difficulties every half hour or so. More to the point, a minor miracle has occurred in that she said I can keep my earnings. All of them!

Mrs Barnes, the pub owner, introduces me to Derek, the chef. Derek smiles and extends a friendly hand but I notice his nails are a bit dirty and there are a few warts on his fingers. I make a mental note never to eat anything from The Duck Revived but to heartily recommend its culinary delights to Mr Cain, my maths teacher.

"And this is Michelle," says Mrs Barnes, grabbing the arm of a passing angel.

"Michelle is our waitress. She's very popular with the clientele."

Looking at Michelle's perfect figure and model-like features, I can see why. She is definitely potential girlfriend material.

"This is Joshua," Mrs Barnes says. "He's going to be helping out every Saturday. Washing the dishes and putting out the rubbish."

Great introduction, Mrs Barnes. Thanks for that.

Michelle looks at me briefly (i.e. the way all girls look at me) before disappearing back into the pub. *Michelle, ma belle*, I hum to myself. Jeez! I make another mental note to bring headphones next week so I don't start corrupting my musical tastes by randomly singing old Beatles' songs. Or worse still, Country and Western, which the Duck seems to have on 24/7.

Mrs Barnes hands me an apron, before droning on a bit more. Allegedly, if I prove reliable in the plate-cleaning department I can advance onto more sophisticated tasks such as taking people's orders and assembling salad garnishes! The anticipation is almost too much for me.

7.30pm: sink

Jesus, "Stand by your Man" is a very catchy song. If I sing it once more I may have to stick an unwashed fork in my eye. Music like that should come with a health warning.

"WARNING: This dross is weirdly addictive and may seriously damage your brain and make you want to take up lassoing for a hobby."

Mrs Barnes swoops in from the bar to inspect my handiwork.

"Did you rinse these?" she asks, pointing at the stacked plates.

"Absolutely," I say.

She runs a finger across one and I feel strangely anxious. I try to read her expression but she's giving nothing away. After an uncomfortable few seconds, she nods and says, "Carry on."

"Thanks," I gush. "Thanks very much!"

God, what is wrong with me? Why do I give a dry roasted peanut what Mrs Barnes thinks? I am starved of affection is what it is. I desperately need a girlfriend! Michelle, do you know how happy I'd be if you were just to make eye contact? Just registering my existence would make me delirious with pleasure.

Michelle appears and dumps a pile of gravy-soaked plates on the draining board. It'll have to do for now.

10.45pm

Finally, I can leave. Mrs Barnes passes me some greasy five pound notes. She looks sneaky and I realise this is what people mean when they say "cash-in-hand". I nod back in a similarly sneaky way and go outside to check my earnings.

Fifteen quid. Fifteen rotten quid! I'm never gonna be able to afford the wondrous Jackson at this rate.

Of course, I could always ask for some more shifts. About a million more!

Or... and here's a thought, I could sell my body! It's not much but it's gotta be worth a few quid to someone. If they didn't want it for sex, I could sell them a lung or something. Do people sell lungs?

Sunday 9th February

9.45am: kitchen

Mum has given me an old pickle jar to put my earnings in and I have just written a label for it:

Jackson Guitar Fund
Not to be touched under pain of death! Seriously!!

I am just about to stick it on the jar when Mum asks me to go to the Parkinsons' next door and feed their cat.

"What's it worth?" I say, pointing to the jar.

Mum gives me one of her exasperated looks. She has no sense of humour whatsoever.

'Get round there right now, young man," she says, lobbing the key at my face.

My mother can be quite scary at times. It's very difficult to stand up to her even though I am about three foot taller than she is. My sister is the same, and my nan too come to think of it. Trust me to be born into a family of psychotic female dwarfs. No wonder Dad went off to work on the rigs.

I feel sad thinking about Dad, so I polish his photo with my sleeve and troop next door.

Wow! It's hard to believe this house is the mirror image of ours. It's so incredibly... tasteful! Everything is painted beige and the TV is huge! Ours is huge too but it's huge depth-ways, which obviously doesn't count.

Jasper the cat is very pleased to see me. His purring is so loud t's like a low-level earthquake (about 3.2 on the Richter scale). I give him a tin of Whiskas and then some vintage Camembert and slices of finest wafer-thin salmon that I find in the fridge. It's not like any of it's gonna be any good when the Parkinsons get back from holiday.

Jasper follows me all the way home. He seems really attached to me. I have quite a way with animals, I think.

10.00pm: front room, on internet

People do not sell lungs, at least not in this country. They probably do in places like Cambodia but it'd cost the price of a lung to get there.

Monday 10th February

3.55pm: Inner Sanctum

Yes! My "Icons of Metal" magazine has arrived. (The subscription was a Christmas present from my nan. I told her it was about science and would be useful for my GCSEs.) This issue is a Black Metal special. There's a great article on pinch harmonics, an anthology of black metal bands and a centre-spread of some girl draped over an amp with not much on (the girl, not the amp). I would like to put the centre-spread up on my wall but my mum's head would probably start rotating and spit would fly out of her mouth so I put it under my mattress instead.

At the back of the magazine are adverts for up-and-coming gigs. Why I torture myself looking at these is anyone's guess. Firstly, I cannot afford to go; secondly, I don't have anyone to go with; and thirdly, most of them seem to be in places like Slovenia. You can imagine my mum's comments if I suggested going there for a holiday:

"If we ever have enough money to go on holiday, Joshua, which I severely doubt given our Financial Difficulties, I shall go to the Costa Del Boring. I shall certainly not go to a place where there might be fascinating folklore, stunning scenery and amazing nightlife."

Anyway, because I'm a masochist I read through the pages and note that Satanic Warmaster are gigging in London in July, which would be perfect for celebrating after the exams. Why, oh why do my friends have such rubbish taste in music?

I also see that Children of Bodom are doing an album signing in Glasgow on Saturday 11th July, a week after my 16th birthday! Glasgow, that's only about 300 miles away. Number 3 on my list could finally be in reach. Ah shut up, Josh, you are delusional.

Tuesday 11th February

4.55pm: front room

I accept two Facebook friend requests – Furkid Furbaby and Hug-a-woozel. They seem like nice ferrets.

Wednesday 12th February

2.25pm: queuing outside Lower Dungeons (AKA English Room E12)

Lydia and her friend Becky Calbag are discussing all the Valentine's cards they expect to receive.

"Are you sending any, Josh?" Becky says with what I assume is sarcasm.

"No," I say. I wanted to reply with some witty put-down but words failed me.

"Like anyone would want one from that knobhead," sneers Lydia.

Words never fail her, unfortunately.

Thursday 13th February

8.10pm: Scouts

We are making Valentine's cards for that special person in our lives.

"Don't worry if you still don't have a girlfriend," Shaun says. "Just give it to someone you care about."

"Who you gonna give yours to?" I ask Peter.

"Probably my mum," he says. "How about you?"

"Definitely not my mum," I say. "I suppose I could give it to this girl I met at the Duck."

"Oh really! Tell me more," says Peter, eyes glinting.

He looks so eager that I feel I have to impress him. "She's a waitress," I say. "Although she's only doing it in-between modelling jobs."

"Modelling? Wow! What sort of modelling does she do?"

"Lingerie, I think. Swimwear, thongs, that kinda thing."

I feel terrible telling such a big lie but there's no going back now. Peter watches closely while I write "To Dear Michelle" in the card and on the envelope. Luckily Ozzy can't read.

Friday 14th February

8.15pm: Inner Sanctum

I've received precisely zero Valentine's cards. What a surprise!

There again there were no offers to arrange my funeral expenses or test-drive the latest Zimmer frame, so I guess I should be grateful for that.

Saturday 15th February

8.25am: Transept to Forbidding Portal (AKA hallway)

Receive an invitation to look round the show home for some newly built retirement flats.

Sunday 16th February

1.30pm: Nan's kitchen

If I didn't go round my nan's for a decent meal every now and then I think I would be seriously malnourished. My mother says she's too busy to cook but I notice she's never too busy to read her trashy magazines. Nan is my only remaining grandparent; both Dad's parents died when I was a kid (not a very long-lived family).

Nan pours gravy on my roast potatoes and I almost swoon, the smell is so good. This is probably the nearest I'll ever get to a drug-induced high.

Nan is a great cook but I worry about her sometimes because she seems a bit confused and forgetful. When she let me in, for example, I swear she called me Jessica. I have no idea who Jessica is, but presumably she's female, so that's a bit odd.

Her memory for things in the past is spookily good, though. She can remember word for word, pointless conversations with her neighbours back in the eighties. I head her off from rattling on about the day Mrs Broughton's prize-winning orchids developed stem rot by bringing up a subject closer to my heart.

"You know my dad," I say.

"Mmm," says Nan.

"Well, what was he like? I mean, really?"

Nan looks awkward. I sometimes get the suspicion she doesn't like talking about her son-in-law much.

"He was very nice," she says after a while. "Very handsome and polite: the strong, silent type."

"Was he like me?" I ask.

"Um, not really dear."

Nan must see I look put out, so she adds, "At least not in looks. Your sister resembles him more in looks. You take after your mum."

Great!

"She was very pretty at your age, your mum," adds Nan, smiling.

Yes, Nan, but maybe I don't want to look pretty!

10.35pm: Inner Sanctum

I've just finished a session at the Duck. I asked Mrs Barnes about extra shifts but she said the woman who does the washing up on the other days needs the money for her starving family in the Philippines. I felt like saying, "Yes, well, I need the money for the epically awesome Jackson!" But I doubt she'd have been sympathetic.

Michelle had her hair up in a high bunch, or what my sister calls a Croydon face-lift. On Michelle it looked stunning. There again, she could wear one of Mum's disgusting brown cardigans and look stunning. I wonder if I should have risked giving her that Valentine's card. I mean, nothing ventured, nothing gained and all that, but no, she probably got loads; just about everyone in the pub thinks she's the best thing since Dolly Parton.

Monday 17th February

7.15pm: Inner Sanctum

I take a short break from doing press-ups and practising "One" by Metallica (not at the same time!) to check in my leather-bound notebook for the list of things to achieve before I'm sixteen.

I have done none of them. Zero. Zilch. Not a one.

If I don't get a girlfriend soon (number 1 on the list) I may have to resort to drastic measures like surgery (me) or hypnosis (them).

I do have £41.10 in the Guitar Fund though.

Tuesday 18th February

6.30pm: Inner Sanctum

Davey phones to ask me over. He needs my graphical skills on Photoshop so he can get a flattering profile picture for Facebook. In particular, he'd like his nose reduced.

I say, "Davey, unfortunately I don't think my skills, impressive as they are, are quite up to that."

Silence.

"Just kidding, Davey," I say. "My Photoshop skills are second to none!"

At least Davey makes an effort in the looks department. Ollie once had a piece of salami in his hair for three whole days.

Thursday 20th February

11.35am: Geography

I am having a brilliant metal-stardom daydream (receiving an award for fastest shredder in the universe) when someone chucks a piece of paper at the back of my head. It says "J 4 B??" on it. What the hell does that mean? Clearly, the person who threw that wants to get me into trouble. I'm already on a warning in Geography for splashing Pot Noodle on my volcano assignment.

I screw up the paper and throw it in the bin. Ha, loser! You'll have to do more than that to get me a detention!

Friday 21st February

8.30pm: Inner Sanctum

I can now do 40 press-ups without collapsing on the point of cardiac arrest. My arm muscles remain as pathetically non-existent as ever though. FML!

Saturday 22nd February

7.00pm: Duck

Dead Duck is dead boring tonight. Michelle has the flu so Mrs Barnes is being waitress, and boy is she a flirt. She sucks up to anyone male and younger than 80 like a turbo-charged Dyson.

"Missing Michelle?" asks Derek.

"Nope," I say, but it's kinda obvious I'm lying.

Monday 24th February

7.30am: Inner Sanctum

My hated alarm goes off and I jump out of bed and reach for my trousers, but then I remember it's half-term!

Yes! A lie-in.

7.35am

Ozzy has escaped his cage and invaded the sacred resting place of my inner sanctum (aka bed). I try burrowing under the duvet but he digs me out with his velociraptor claws. It's no good I'll have to feed him. FMLx2!

Tuesday 25th February

2.30pm: Mr Pitman's

Mr Pitman is not feeling good today. When I pass him his tea I notice his fingers look very gnarly. He must see me looking because he says, "You know, I once had really nimble fingers. They used to call me nimble-fingered Ned!"

"Really," I say. "That's an unusual name."

"Make the most of your youth lad," Mr Pitman goes on. "It's over all too quickly."

Fortunately, Mr Pitman does not say: these are the best days of your life etc., etc., so I don't have to go find some high-voltage jump leads. Instead, I assure Mr Pitman that I will try and make the most of my youth, although it seems bloody difficult what with having to go to school, do homework, do other people's homework, make my tea, feed Ozzy, walk people's dogs, slave away in the local pub, check Facebook, and generally cope with the pile of rubbish that is my life. I don't tell him all that last bit. He looks depressed enough already.

"OK," I say to Minty once we're outside. "We do guitar for me, then park for you. Fair?"

Minty squats to do a pee, which I take as a yes.

Minty and me go and see my guitar. She is looking lovely as ever (the guitar not Minty – Minty looks OK). Anyway, I want to get a closer look so I tie Minty to Steve's Emporium's drainpipe and go in.

"Nice-looking guitar, that," says Steve. I know it's him as he has a badge saying "Steve" on. "Wanna try her out?"

I can hardly believe my luck. Of course, I want to. There again, what am I going to play? "Spanish Romance" is out, that's for sure. I see a few other guys in the shop looking at me. The pressure is on!

"Just have a play around," suggests Steve. "Knock yourself out."

Luckily, my hands seem to have worked out what to do, which is good since my brain is being useless as usual. I hammer out a few AC/DC riffs, a decent metal gallop and some bars of "Paranoid" by Black Sabbath. My pentatonic is blisteringly fast and before long, the other guys in the shop have come over and are nodding their heads. Is this what it feels like to play a solo live in front of 20,000 screaming fans?

Well, no, but it feels quite nice.

Suddenly, all eyes turn from me to outside the shop. Jeez, there's a hell of a rumpus out there – sounds like some kind of dog fght... Some kind of dog fight!

I hand the guitar over to one of the nodding dudes and rush outside where I am amazed to see Minty attacking Ollie's labrador, Bongo.

"Stop that, Minty!" I yell, and miraculously she obeys and lets Borgo hide behind Ollie's legs.

"God," says Ollie. "You never told me you'd got a dog."

"She's not mine," I say. "I walk her for Mr Pitman."

"She's f***ing mental!"

"I know," I say.

"Mr Pitman?" muses Ollie. "Ain't he that guy whose wife ran off with the Tesco delivery man?"

"I dunno," I say. "He did get divorced last year."

"Yeah, my gran lives down his road and she said Mrs Pitman used to disappear into the Tesco van for hours. My gran was disgusted. She said it was no wonder the bread was always squashed."

"Poor Mr Pitman," I say. "I never knew that."

"He should've set her on them," says Ollie, nodding towards Minty. "Imagine them gnashers clamped round yer knackers."

Um, I'd rather not, thanks, Ollie.

Wednesday 26th February

10.20am: Inner Sanctum

Spurred on by yesterday's success at Steve's Emporium, I spend the morning designing stage sets for my band in my leather-bound notebook. I have loads of cool ideas:

1. TVs all over the stage, on the amps and the drum riser. The TVs could have static like in that Japanese horror film.

2. Cut-outs of broken-down buildings, bricks, broken glass and bits of barbed wire.

3. Wax models - really creepy ones!

4. Stuffed animals, bits of old trees and vines wrapping round the lights - possible fire risk but good to play on people's interest in the environment.

I would like to go on, but I have masses of homework that I ought to be doing as per usual. I open up my French book and find that I have to write about my town, its facilities and what would make it better. How do you say "a nuclear bomb" in French?

11.15pm

Just remembered it's Mum's birthday tomorrow. I will have to raid the Guitar Fund to get her something. God damn it. How am I ever going to be able to afford the wondrous Jackson if I have to keep buying people presents?

11.20pm

On the other hand, I could make her something out of things I find discarded in the house. That'll cost nothing and be far more thoughtful.

Thursday 27th February – Mum's birthday

4.00pm: Cinema, watching the film *Up*

Oh my God, this film is so sad; I'm having to work hard at not blubbing. In fact, I am blubbing. Beside me, Maddie is also dabbing her eyes and wiping away snot. Mum, however, remains dry-eyed and stony-faced. I am now more convinced than ever that she is a robot.

She liked the cardboard peg holder I made her though.

Friday 28th February

8.00pm: Davey's house for sleepover

Another birthday today – this time Davey's. His mum and dad have bought him a laptop, an iPad, Nike trainers and a Ferrari. Not a real Ferrari, but a cake in the shape of one. All of this kind of puts the can of Boots shaving foam I got him in the shade. Still, you can't shave with an iPad.

Or can you?

8.10pm: Davey's Inner Sanctum

I am so stuffed with pizza, Coke and Ferrari, I can hardly move. I gotta say, Davey sure knows how to pack the grub away. Currently he is tucking into yet another family bag of tangy cheese Doritos.

"Jesus, Davey," I say. "If eating ever becomes an Olympic sport, you'll be a triple gold medallist!"

"Thanks," says Davey, putting the packet down.

Davey is one of those kids blessed with normal parents, i.e. parents who let him have a TV, Xbox, PlayStation, DVD player and computer in his own room. We are playing "Call of Duty" and I am letting the team down badly. This is what happens when you don't have the latest stuff at home to practise on. I should sue my mum for emotional, physical and technological neglect.

2.15am: still in Davey's Inner Sanctum with lights out

As usual, I'm the only one still awake. It's hard to get comfy because Davey keeps flapping his arms in my face and Ollie keeps farting. The last one smelt so bad I'm amazed it didn't corrode a hole in his sleeping bag. Meanwhile, Peter's phone keeps blinking and buzzing. Will I get any sleep tonight?

5.30am

No.

Saturday 29th February

Sleeping – Guitar – Duck – Sleeping.

Sunday 1st March

Sleeping – Guitar – Ozzy – Sleeping.
One of my better weekends. :)

Monday 2nd March

6.00pm: Inner Sanctum

I should be doing some weight training but I can't be arsed. I just don't think I have the type of body that puts on muscle. Really, I should stop being so pathetically shallow and learn to be happy with my physique the way it is.

6.05pm

I wonder if you can get bicep implants...

Tuesday 3rd March

4.15pm: Throne Room (AKA bathroom) scrubbing Ozzy's cage

Ozzy's cage is now sparkling but there is a problem. It seems that if you put vast quantities of sawdust down a toilet, the toilet stops working. Ozzy and me watch as the water swirls around, rising frighteningly high up the sides like a big pot of boiling... sawdust.

"Shit," I say.

Ozzy looks at me with his beady eyes and says, "Dook?"

"You'll be alright," I say. "Mum likes *you*."

4.35pm

I have managed to get the toilet working again but it required drastic action and I am slightly traumatised.

Wednesday 4th March – 4 months till my 16th birthday

8.20am: Transept to Forbidding Portal

I receive a free sample of deluxe, ultra-absorbent incontinence pads through the post. This has gone too far now. I will have to complain to the postman.

It's four months till my birthday, so I still have four months to get a girlfriend, see Children of Bodom live, learn "One" by Metallica, get a piercing and/or tattoo, metamorphose into someone cool and strong like my dad and save up for the wondrous Jackson.

Four months suddenly doesn't seem very long.

Thursday 5th March

7.30pm: Scouts

"Tonight we have a music quiz!" cries Shaun. (He is very easily excited.) "I'm sure you'd all like to thank Jess and Lucy for organising it."

Jess and Lucy wear pink hair bands and giggle a lot, which isn't a good sign IMHO. Note to self: they are definitely not potential girlfriend material.

I team up with Peter, hoping he will field the questions on pop, and with Nick Armstrong because he has no one else to go with, largely because he never stops picking his nose. Anyway, not surprisingly, we do crap because there are no questions on Susan Boyle and none on metal. What sort of music quiz is this? It's a crap music quiz is the answer.

I complain to Shaun and he says that he's surprised I didn't get the question on U2 as I am such a guitar buff (as he calls it). Shaun goes on to state that The Edge is probably the world's best ever guitar player.

I disagree, saying, "Ah, but can he play at 280 beats per minute for longer than five minutes at a time?"

Shaun starts to answer but I interject. "Can he play while simultaneously singing and leaping off a car?"

"How should I know?" says Shaun irritably.

"Alexi Laiho from Children of Bodom can," I say.

Shaun then pretends to be busy adjusting the scarf of one of the younger Scouts. He is quite a sore loser.

10.10pm: Inner Sanctum

I'm wondering if I should have been nicer to Shaun about The Edge. I shall probably never receive my Musician's badge now.

Friday 6th March

8.30pm: kitchen

I am exhausted. First, I walked Minty, then I had to walk Mrs Harris's tiny orange Poodle, Cindy-Lou. I was dreading seeing someone from school so kept to the back roads, but who should come round the corner of Dukes Avenue but the Lovely (Not) Lydia and her BFF Becky.

"Hi Josh," said Becky, "Nice dog."

Yeah, yeah, very funny!

I pulled up my jacket collar, kept my head down and hurried

on, pretending not to know them. I have a painful bruise from walking into a parking meter, but at least I got £5 from Mrs Harris. Mrs Harris thinks I'm a "lovely young man". Unfortunately, she is over eighty and hence not potential girlfriend material.

Guitar Fund now stands at £96.92 plus 3 euros and a green button. I have no idea where the button came from but unless it's worth £400, I am still a million miles from the Jackson.

Saturday 7th March

6.10pm: Throne Room

It's Saturday, which means, joy of joys, my weekly torture at The Duck Revived. If I had my way, the duck would've been left to breathe its last and die with dignity. Anyway, while other teenagers are out kissing in bus shelters and generally having an amazing time, I will be up to my elbows in soap suds and, if I'm really lucky, allowed to arrange some lettuce.

I should be getting ready for work but instead I remain sat on the toilet, listening to the melodic tones of Cannibal Corpse on my headphones. I let my eyes glaze over and the clutter of the bathroom blurs out of focus. All my sister's sprays, lotions and balms recede from view. Where does she get the energy to care about things like brittle cuticles, I wonder?

I'm starting to feel dozy but suddenly the door creaks open, which panics me into action. Thankfully, it's only Ozzy (escaped from his cage again). Ozzy rolls around happily in the toilet paper.

"Ozzy, you are my one true mate," I tell him.

"Dook. Dook," agrees Ozzy.

"Promise me you'll never leave."

"Dook. Dook."

"There's a prom after the exams," I go on. "It's ages away yet but what if I'm the only one without a girlfriend? True, none of my mates have girlfriends, but Ollie and Davey are rich and will be able to bribe someone to go with them and Peter is almost certainly gay."

6.15pm

Maybe I should say I'm gay. A gay metalhead? Well, the guy from Judas Priest pulled it off. (Being gay that is, not his head.)

No, that would be suicide; boys might come onto me. Peter might come onto me!

"Ah God, what should I do Ozzy? Give me the benefit of your ferrety wisdom."

Ozzy jumps up on my lap but his paws get caught in the leads from my headphones and he loses his footing, sending a long bloody scrape down my thigh. It'll probably leave quite an impressive scar. Shame no one will ever see it.

"Josh," calls Mum. "What are you doing up there? It's twenty past six; you'll be late for work."

Well, it's another £15 I suppose. I wipe off the blood and get changed. At the bottom of the stairs I check the picture of Dad on the cabinet. Dad is leaning on a gate somewhere, probably Scotland. He is very good looking. Even though I am definitely not gay, I can see that. And his arms are even bigger than Clint's! One thing's for sure, I will never be half as strong or cool as he was.

6.35pm: Duck Revived

At the pub, Mrs Barnes looks me up and down, walks round me still looking me up and down and then says: "Hmm. Yes, OK."

Mrs Barnes believes I am presentable enough to be seen mingling amongst the prestigious (not!) clientele of The Duck Revived. However, my duties are strictly limited.

"Taking orders is harder than it looks," she tells me. "I'm not sure we should let you loose on that just yet. But I don't see why you can't go and collect people's dirty plates."

Wow! Thanks, I say, it'll be brain surgery next!

Actually, I just nod. I haven't the energy for anything else. Somehow working at the Duck robs me of the will to string a sensible sentence together. Anyway, it'll give me a chance to lose the gloves I'd started wearing. I've noticed a bit of a rash developing on my wrist, suggesting I'm allergic to rubber. This probably cuts a whole sphere of potentially interesting experimentation out of my future sex life. Assuming I have a future sex life! Deep sea diving is probably a no-no, too.

The Duck Revived used to be a laid-back working man's pub but Mrs Barnes has decided to change all that and "revamp it". She shows me the new menu, which has been cobbled together in Microsoft Word and has clip art pictures of smiling cutlery.

"My nephew did this," she says. "He's only about your age but he's incredibly clever with computers."

"I can tell," I say.

Instead of chips, we now sell Pommes Frites with garlic mayo. Instead of cheese and tomato rolls, we have toasted paninis with buffalo mozzarella and roasted vegetables.

Derek, for one, is not happy. "I can't even pronounce this menu," he moans.

I sympathise, but at least my job of making the salad garnishes has got a bit more interesting. I have to grate carrot now and twist the cucumber slices into little "s" shapes. If we're not too busy, I may even cut little "v"s into the tomato halves. Then again, I may come to my senses.

"Table 3," instructs Mrs Barnes. "Quickly, Joshua, we don't want the flies landing."

I clip my heels together and salute her retreating back, which amuses Derek for some reason. I leave him coughing and spluttering into the deep-fat fryer and head out into the pub.

God, it's amazing what people leave on their plates. I'm tempted to pick on some leftover cheese, but Mrs Barnes is watching me like a vulture from the bar. I can feel her eyes stripping the skin from my bones.

Michelle whisks by with a tray, calling out, "Table 12, three tuna paninis, one bean jacket."

Somehow, she manages to make the job look sexy. And it seems I'm not the only one to think so. I hear the recipients, a group of about four blokes, calling her "darling" and stuff.

Jeez! One of them sounded just like that moron my sister calls a boyfriend, otherwise known as Clint.

I look around cautiously.

It *is* Clint!

I scurry back with my dirty plates. If that lowlife spots me, I'll never hear the end of it.

Michelle follows me into the kitchen, looking pink and cross.

"Jerk," she says.

I apologise but she says she doesn't mean me. Apparently, one of the blokes at table 12 pinched her bottom and said that he'd pay her to give him a lap dance.

What a disgusting thing to say. Men like that should be ashamed of themselves.

10.30pm

As I walk home, I wonder if Michelle's sexual harasser was Clint. I wouldn't be surprised, the guy's a jerk and it's not just me who thinks so; Mum doesn't rate him much either. Anyway, whoever it was, that really was out of order talking about a lap dance. Although I can imagine Michelle might be quite good at one. She certainly has the figure...

Sunday 8th March

10.10am: kitchen

I come downstairs to find Mr Coles from over the road fixing our freezer. There are packets of soggy vegetables and fish fingers all over the floor.

"What ho, lad," says Mr Coles, laying down his screwdriver. "Got a girlfriend yet?"

What is it with these people? They are more obsessed with me finding a girlfriend than I am.

"He's concentrating on his studies," says Mum proudly.

"Ah," says Mr Coles. "I should've done that, but at his age I was out on the town, living it up. Best days of my life, they were."

"Oh yes, mine too," says Mum with a weird twinkle in her eye.

I wonder how easy it is to kill two people with a screwdriver and a bag of half-frozen peas. I decide to go back upstairs before the darker side of me attempts to find out.

Monday 9th March

8.15am: front door

Our Postman tells me I have made his day when I complain about the pensioner mail I've been getting. He is laughing so much, it looks like he's about to wet himself.

Perhaps if he does, he'll be more understanding about my incontinence pads.

6.45pm: kitchen

My sister is getting trained in ear piercing at Fringe Benefits, the hairdressers where she works.

"Great!" I say. "You can do mine."

"You are not having your ears pierced!" announces Mum with such venom it's like I've asked if I can open a topless bar in the front room.

"Loads of people have pierced ears, Mum," I say. "You have!"

"I'm a girl," says Mum.

Er, Mum, sorry to disappoint you but you stopped being a girl about thirty years ago.

"Promise me you won't pierce his ears, Maddie," Mum goes on.

"I promise," says my pathetic, goody two-shoes, pathetic wimp of a sister.

Tuesday 10th March

12.40pm: astroturf

"So," says Ollie. "Anyone receive any interesting mail recently?"

"Not me," says Peter.

"Nah," says Davey. "All I ever get is offers on extreme sports holidays and fast cars. You know – young people kind of mail."

"Yeah, me too," says Ollie. "Still, better that than getting a load of mail targeted at really old people or people with embarrassing health conditions!"

"What is that girl wearing?" I say, pointing to some run-of-the-mill Year 7 kid in completely normal school uniform.

I had to change the subject quickly – couldn't let them know I've been receiving incontinence pads through the post.

Wednesday 11th March

4.30pm: car park outside Music Block

I suggest to Mr Trumper that music would be more popular at GCSE if people could study the various genres and sub-genres of metal along with the classics, world music, etc.

Mr Trumper said metal probably wasn't influential enough as a genre.

I said, on the contrary, that with their roots in the blues and psychedelic rock the first metal bands such as Sabbath and Deep Purple were greatly influential. With their amplified distortion, extended solos, and basic all-round loudness they went on to inspire multiple genres such as punk, grunge and even new wave.

Furthermore, they spawned a variety of sub-genres including but not limited to: thrash, typified by bands such as Metallica; glam rock, typified by Mötley Crüe; black metal, typified by Mayhem; and death metal, typified by Slayer and Morbid Angel. Death metal in turn has a number of sub-sub-genres, including melodic death metal, typified by Children of Bodom. Plus there's melodic metal core and melodic death core of course.

Mr Trumper said that he really had to go now as he'd left the iron in the oven but he'd certainly suggest it to the examining board.

It'll be too late for me, but I feel I have done a good deed for all future metalheads considering their options at GCSE.

11.10pm: Inner Sanctum

Iron in the oven?

Thursday 12th March

3.50pm: walking home from school

"So, you're really gonna do it," says Ollie.

"Yes," I say. "Probably tomorrow evening when Mum's round Nan's."

"But won't she be a bit, er, cross?" says Ollie.

"Incandescent with rage," I say.

"That's what I thought," says Ollie. "Mate, you are looking

63

death in the face."

"Look," I say, "I am nearly sixteen, Mum has to accept that she can't control every little aspect of my life."

"Hmm," says Ollie.

10.00pm: Inner Sanctum

Death holds no fear

For a warrior king

His skin pierced all over

With stud, spike and ring

From the album: *Looking Death in the Face* by Josh Walker

Friday 13th March – unlucky for some! Me, probably.

6.15pm: Inner Sanctum

"Are you sure you don't want to come and see Nan?" says Mum.

"Sorry," I say. "I would, but I've got loads of homework."

"We can always go a bit later," says Mum. "Will you have finished in an hour?"

I shake my head. "No, sorry. Really have got loads."

"And you have to finish it all tonight?"

"'Fraid so."

"Well, OK then."

Finally, Mum leaves. I listen for the front door closing, then run to the window and watch her strutting up the road. Great. She should be gone at least two hours, which means I have plenty of time to do the deed!

6.45pm: bathroom

Eagerly I open up my sister's piercing kit and look inside. It seems kinda complicated. There are lots of pieces and the needle itself looks a bit scary, kind of like a giant stapler.

Hmm. Maybe I should play some guitar to chill me out before getting started. I've got plenty of time after all.

7.00pm: Inner Sanctum

I'm just getting to grips with my "One" Metallica tab when there's a loud scream from the landing.

"Please, Josh," my sister says. "It's huge."

"What is?" I say.

My sister points to her bedroom floor.

"Oh," I say, putting the guitar aside.

"Urgh, it's massive, Josh," says my sister, going into a shivering spasm.

I look down at the admittedly pretty damn enormous spider and then, for some reason, my eyes are drawn to a pile of my sister's clothes on her floor...

"I will remove it and deposit it outside," I say, "if you agree to do something for me. If you don't agree, I will deposit it in your underwear drawer."

I surprise myself with my wickedness. My voice turned kind

of "evil scientist".

Maddie regards me with a mixture of horror and loathing, i.e. fairly normally.

"You wouldn't," she says.

"You know, I think it's a tarantula," I say. "This one is so big she could be pregnant. They love soft cosy places to nest, or so I've heard, places like... knickers."

My sister looks like she's about to cry and I feel a bit ashamed, but I can't weaken now. "Apparently, they have six million babies," I say.

"What d'you want me to do?" she moans.

I point to her piercing kit on the bathroom cabinet.

"But I promised Mum I wouldn't touch your ears."

"Who said anything about my ears?" I say.

"Not your penis!"

"No, not my penis! Jesus! It's my eyebrow. I want you to pierce my eyebrow."

My sister reluctantly agrees, although she will only do it after I have got rid of the spider. She follows me downstairs at a safe distance and watches me deposit it over the neighbour's wall. Then she turns, legs it upstairs like Usain Bolt and locks herself in the bathroom.

"Sorry Josh," she cries, "but Mum would kill me. You know how she is about stuff like that. Oh, and by the way, your eyebrows are kinda bushy. You don't really wanna draw attention to them."

FML!

Sunday 15th March

11.20 am: bathroom

Bushy? They are certainly not bushy. I think the word my sister was looking for was manly.

Monday 16th March

12.30pm: sat on astroturf with Davey

"Do you think my eyebrows are bushy?" I ask Davey.

"Well, stop moving them up and down and I'll tell you," he says.

I halt my wayward brows and try to look normal(ish). "Well?"

"They're fine."

"Not a bit on the fuzzy caterpillar side?"

"They're fine!"

"OK. Thanks. What you got for lunch?" Normally Davey's mum makes him some kind of three-course, Michelin-star banquet for lunch.

"Nothing," says Davey

"Oh hey," I say. "Want some crisps?"

"No, I don't," says Davey. "And why do you always have smoky bacon crisps, they stink the place out."

"I thought you liked smoky bacon," I say.

"Not anymore," says Davey.

"Right."

Davey sighs. "Is it too much," he says, "to want to be respected and liked for who I am?"

"Er, well in your case, probably," I say.

"Thanks!" says Davey, getting up. "Thanks a lot!"

"I was joking, Davey," I say. "I like you. And, er, respect you..."

But he doesn't come back.

10.05pm: Inner Sanctum

Guitar Fund is at £144.76. It's no good. I will have to find another way to earn some money.

Tuesday 17th March

1.10pm: astroturf

Davey's off from school today. It sounds mean, but I can't say I'm sorry; he's been in a really bad mood recently.

I ask Ollie how he gets money and he says, "I'm a paid sex slave."

"You wish," I say.

"Actually," he says. "My parents just kinda give me it, but you could always get a paper round."

A paper round! Why didn't I think of it before?

Wednesday 18th March

I'm quite excited about the paper round. I can imagine myself striding out in the early morning sunshine, birds tweeting (singing, not typing short computer updates), wind in my hair, headphones on full blast. I decide to call in at Hooper's newsagents on the way back from school.

4.20pm: Hooper's

I ask Mr Hooper if he has any openings for a paper boy.

Mr Hooper looks me up and down and says, "Is this the sort of job you see yourself doing in three years time?"

"Well, um, not really," I say. "I'll probably be in college then, or university maybe..."

"Forget it then," he says. "There's a three-year waiting list."

Thursday 19th March

7.20pm: Scouts

Shaun is very excited this evening because it's just two days after St Patrick's Day. He says we are going to celebrate in a traditional Irish way. Unfortunately, this is not by drinking large amounts of Guinness.

7.40pm

Shaun accuses Peter of not being a team player because he refuses to let some younger scouts cover his head in green paint. Peter says green is not his colour and goes off to sulk with his phone.

I am quite enjoying being painted though, mainly because the painter is Stephanie Nagle who, though not Michelle quality, is definitely potential girlfriend material. It's kind of like having a head massage, except for getting the occasional bit of paint in the eyes, nose and mouth. Stephanie gives me a big smile and I'm wondering if I should risk asking her out. Rejection would be mortifying, but I'm never going to achieve number 1 on the list if I don't take some risks. Besides, I have this sneaky feeling she may find me quite attractive.

"So, Stephanie..." I begin.

"Yikes!" she announces, stepping back. "It's the green goblin off Spiderman!"

Friday 20th March

9.00pm: Inner Sanctum writing in my leather-bound notebook

I've been working on a stage name and have decided that Josh the Destroyer captures my personality pretty well. But how should I write it?

1. JOSH THE DESTROYER

2. Josh the Destroyer

3. Josh the Destroyer

4. JOSH THE DESTROYER

5. JOSH THE DESTROYER

I think I like number five the best, plus it has the advantage of being almost impossible to read. NB: the more illegible the logo, the more metal the band!

Saturday 21st March

8.50pm: Duck

I'm on cloud 10 tonight. Michelle has just come and told me my salad garnishes are really professional looking.

I thought at first she was taking the piss but then Derek came and said "Jeez mate, you're too good to work 'ere. Them's Mitchelin tyre quality, them."

Maybe I should be a chef when I grow up?

No, I must stand firm: It's Guitar God or death.

I was born to set the axe on fire

Make it scream with wild desire

Pain and fury caressing the frets

Growling sounds like a kid with Tourette's

From the album: *Guitar God or Death* by Josh the Destroyer

Sunday 22nd March

3.15pm: Inner Sanctum

Ollie has come over so we can do our maths together. We reckon Mr Cain must've been in one hell of a mood to set such a lot. There are four A4 sheets of equations to fill in.

"Jesus," says Ollie, eyeing the questions. "These are friggin' hard."

The questions *are* hard. This is going to take hours, but it won't be so bad doing them with a friend.

"You get started on the first one," I say. "I gotta go to the loo."

When I get back I am horrified to see Ollie laid out on my bed looking through my leather-bound notebook!

I feel my heart start to thud and the blood surge to my face.

"What's this?" he says, seeing me. "Why have you written Josh the Destroyer lots of times in weird writing?"

"Give that here," I say, making a lunge.

"And what are all these names?"

"Ollie, give it here!"

I manage to get a hold of the book but Ollie yanks it back and I'm left with one ripped page. This turns out to be a good thing though because Ollie finally stops being a jerk and hands the book over.

"They are names," I say.

"Huh?"

"Of bands."

"I haven't heard of them."

"Of my band. When I get one. If I get one."

"Right," says Ollie thoughtfully. "And Josh the Destroyer?"

"My stage name. I was experimenting with, er, signatures."

Ollie starts to grin. "Like autographs, you mean?"

"Yes, look, you won't, er..."

"Tell anyone? No, no."

"Thanks!" I say. "Thanks very much, Ollie. 'Cause that book's private and..."

"At least not..."

3.30pm

I leave Ollie watching YouTube videos of skateboarding dogs while I do our Maths homework.

All of it.

Or my own.

I cannot believe Ollie thought it was OK to do that. I would never read anyone's private, innermost secrets. Never.

Monday 23rd March

10.35am: The Coliseum (AKA school gym)

I have to play Lydia at table tennis. Lydia fancies herself as a bit of a table tennis guru, so I am going to have to beat her. It may take every ounce of my concentration but I have to do it.

"Come on then," she moans. "Let's get this over."

"Yes, lets," I say.

"Should only take a few minutes," she sneers.

"30 seconds tops," I say. "Hey! I wasn't ready."

"Is it my fault you can't stop talk...? Hey!"

The next few minutes are a blur. Literally. The ball is smashing around the table so fast it's like a sped up cartoon version of table tennis. It's like table tennis at warp speed. Mostly I am matching her point-for-point, but a silly lapse in concentration means she is now serving at game point.

'Go for it, Lids," urges Becky just as Lydia takes the shot. Luckily, it's a rubbish serve and I am able to punish it for all it's worth. Rafael Nadal would have been proud of that smash.

"F**K!" says Lydia. "Becky, you stupid cow, you put me off!"

"Sorry," says Becky.

I serve the next point and win it easily. "Game, set and match," I announce.

I then dance around a bit until Mr Cox notices and orders me down from the table.

6.00pm: kitchen

I am still grinning to myself about PE when my sister puts a downer on things by announcing that she will have to give her piercing kit back as she is being made redundant from Fringe Benefits. Any chance of achieving number 5 on my list is now therefore lost unless she gets a new job as a tattooist, which seems unlikely, given that she's about as artistic as a prawn cracker.

I guess I should be more sympathetic but these are harsh times we are living in. Besides, she has an interview as a junior stylist at Curl Up and Dye next week.

10.40pm: Inner Sanctum

Decide to add Curl Up and Die to my list of band names, but can't find it.

Tuesday 24th March

8.20pm: Inner Sanctum

Ollie texts me to say: "Hey, Josh the Destroyer, how's it going?"

I do not dignify him with a reply. I am still livid at him for reading my diary.

Wednesday 25th March

Yes! My hair now goes past my collar. I make sure to tuck it in every evening before Mum gets in. I can't believe she hasn't noticed, or maybe she's lightening up a bit in her old age.

Nah.

Thursday 26th March

8.55pm: Scouts

We made vegetable curry tonight. Peter's mum bought the ingredients and Peter's mum is not obsessed with getting everything on the cheap, so we had some decent stuff to work with for a change.

I'm getting annoyed with Peter though, because he keeps going off using his phone. God knows what he's doing on it. The games he has are crap. Anyway, I've had to chop all the onions and carrots myself. Stephanie Nagle has smiled at me sympathetically a few times but she is no longer potential girlfriend material, not since the green goblin comment.

Friday 27th March

2.35pm: Tower of Terror

"Sarah Clegg, 28/30. Excellent effort. Well done, Sarah."

Mr Cain is going round the class handing back our homework.

"Andrew Parr, 9/30, disappointing. Remember you need to cancel down fully. Ollie Hargreaves, 30/30. Fantastic, Ollie. That's the best you've done all year!"

Yeah right, I think. Not that he did much of it, actually.

"Joshua Walker, ah yes here's an interesting one. Along with your maths sheets (30/30, I hope you didn't copy off Ollie!) you appear to have submitted a long list of something. I'm not sure what it is. Let's see, now:

Vulgar coffin

Blood Sukerz – note spelling with a "z", it says here

The Axemen Cometh

Josh the Destroyer and the Evil Goats

Er, shall I go on?"

I feel my face go red and my throat go dry. A few people have started to giggle.

"There's more…"

"Er, no sir. Please don't go on," I manage.

"Well, I'm not sure about the rest of the class but I'm intrigued. What's it all about, Josh, eh?"

Saturday 28th March

7.30pm: Duck

Mrs Barnes is making me clean out the bins tonight. They smell worse than Ozzy's litter tray.

I sometimes wonder what Dad is thinking if he's looking down on me. Is he proud or disgusted? Is he impressed at my dogged perseverance or appalled at my ability to sink to any level? I am prostituting my soul for the Jackson. I wish I could prostitute my body, but no one'll take it.

Sunday 29th March

8.30pm: lounge, watching X Factor

Unable to keep things bottled up any longer, I confide in Mum about my epic fail in Maths on Friday.

She is not a bit sympathetic. "The trouble is, Josh, you don't live in the real world," she says, shaking her head.

1.15am: Inner Sanctum

No Mum, the trouble is I do.

Monday 30th March

9.10am: assembly – being stared at (and not in a good way)

It has got around school that I'm a sad loser who makes up crap names for bands. I didn't think my social status could sink any lower but I was wrong. I am the human equivalent of a worm. A parasite that lives in a worm's intestine. A...

No, I think that's it.

Tuesday 31st March

5.40pm: Inner Sanctum

Yes! Just when I thought things were well and truly f****d socially, I have been invited to a party. OK, so the whole class has. Probably the whole year... Probably the whole school, including teachers, teaching assistants, dinner ladies and our ninety-five-year-old caretaker. But at least it's not the whole school except me!

The party is Becky Calbag's 16th and her parents are hiring a hall. Unfortunately, there is going to be a disco, but there is also likely to be alcohol, and even Lady Gaga sounds OK if you're smashed.

I gotta say she didn't give much notice (Becky, not Lady Gaga). The party is on Saturday and astonishingly Mrs Barnes has agreed I can swap my day. I'll have to go shopping tomorrow to get a present. More money from the Guitar Fund! Also, what do you give a teenage girl for her birthday? I have no idea.

6.10pm

My sister pops her head round my door.

"Excuse me, but can you knock?" I say.

"Excuse me, but the door wasn't shut," she says.

"It was very slightly ajar."

My sister does that thing where she closes her eyes, turns her head away and sighs. "Have you seen my new mascara?" she says. "I only just bought it and I can't find it anywhere."

"No," I say. "Close the door on your way out."

Wednesday 1st April

7.10am: Inner Sanctum

"Wake up, Josh," says my sister, shaking me. "It's ten past nine. You're late for school."

"F***!"

I jump out of bed, fling on my clothes, shove some Ferret

Feast in Ozzy's cage and leg it out the door. I can usually make it to school in 10 minutes if I run like hell.

7.25am: school – deserted

I absolutely, positively hate my sister.

6.45pm: Duck

Things are a lot more relaxed in the Duck on a Wednesday. The customers are mostly pensioners and people with small kids rather than young adults. There's more spilt Coke and dropped chips – those old folks have rubbish table manners! But in general, it's about a zillion times nicer. I must ask Mrs Barnes if I can change my night to Wednesday.

7.30pm

Mrs Barnes says, No, I cannot change my night to Wednesday. She needs me when it's nightmarishly hectic, noisy and full of horrible yobs, my words not hers.

Friday 3rd April

4 20pm: lounge

My delightful sister is singing her head off because she has just received a phone call telling her she's been accepted as Junior Stylist at Curl Up and Dye.

6.00pm: Inner Sanctum

My sister's over the top happiness is getting a bit wearing, so I have retreated to my Inner Sanctum. If I'm going to sacrifice my hearing it will be to metal, not my sister's tuneless squawking. Honestly, my family are about as musical as a vegetable pasty. It's a miracle I can play a note.

6.15pm

One day till the party.

Not that I'm excited or anything.

Saturday 4th April – PAR TAY!!!

7.40pm: Inner Sanctum

Seem to remember there might be some kind of party on tonight. Peter's mum is going to pick me up at 8.30, which means I have a bit of time to rock out to some decent music before the "disco dross" infects my brain. I grab the trusty acoustic and fire up some Slayer.

9.00pm: East Surrey Hospital Outpatients Department

"And you say you did this playing the guitar?" says the doctor, looking down at my horribly swollen ankle. "How, exactly?"

"Um."

"He pretends the area between his bed and the wardrobe is a stage and jumps around in it," says my sister gleefully.

"That's ridiculous," I say.

"At last, we agree on something!" announces my sister.

"Well," says the doctor, "you won't be jumping around on that ankle for a while. It's not broken, but it's a nasty sprain. I suggest you sit down somewhere safe next time you want to do some guitar practice."

"Really," says my mother, when the doctor has gone. "You're crazier than the ferret."

"Actually Mum," I say. "It was Ozzy's fault this happened. How was I to know he'd sneaked onto the sta... Under the bed. Um, is he OK?"

"I don't know," says Mum. "I haven't seen him, but I doubt it with 140 pounds of adolescent boy landing on him."

"I didn't land on him," I say. "Well, I may have clipped his tail."

My sister shakes her head and goes off to get a coffee. She is replaced by the nurse, who has arrived to bandage me up. She's not unattractive (the nurse, that is). She's actually quite cute.

"At least it's not broken, eh?" she says.

"Yeah," I nod. "I don't wanna do that again. I broke my other ankle when I was thirteen, falling off my bike."

The nurse smiles. She is very pretty. "I don't know, you teenagers, you're so..."

Wild and reckless?

Brave and impulsive?

"Clumsy and stupid," supplies my mum. "He was riding backwards down the concrete steps outside Marks & Spencers. It's amazing he didn't suffer brain damage. In fact, sometimes I think he has!"

"What's that in your pocket?" says my sister, arriving back on

81

the scene with a coffee for herself and Mum – none for me, the invalid, I note.

I look down, "Oh that, that's..."

"It's my mascara!" she says. "You dirty, lying thief!"

"Um, please sit still," says the nurse.

"Why have you got my mascara?" demands my sister.

"Sorry," I say. "It was for Becky. I didn't know what else…"

My sister storms off in a huff and for some reason I start laughing uncontrollably. "Sorry," I tell the nurse.

"See what I mean," says my mum.

Sunday 5th April – three months till my 16th birthday!

Mum says I have to go to school tomorrow. I am so depressed, I can barely pick up the guitar. It is only one day before the start of the hols but I still have to go because according to my mum, "I may miss something important." Yeah, right.

Monday 6th April

10.25am: Field of Nightmares

No PE for me. No PE for me. Everyone else will get cold and wet but there's no PE for me!

I am in a good mood due to getting a lift to school from my mother (amazingly, she didn't insist I crawl the entire way) and missing PE. There's something excellent about sitting fully clothed at the side of the football pitch watching everyone else freeze to death; it's almost worth spraining your ankle for. But then Ollie spoils things by bringing up the party.

"You missed a great party on Saturday," he says. "Everyone wondered where you were."

"Did they?" I say surprised.

"Well, me and Davey did."

"Great."

"And Becky," adds Peter. "She kept saying, 'When's your skinny friend coming?' "

"Nice," I say. "Can I help it if I'm skinny? I work out, well, used to."

"Maybe you've got a tapeworm," says Ollie, wiggling his finger in my face.

"No," says Peter. "It's in your genes. Some kids are just born sticks. Probably your dad was really thin."

"Actually," I say. "My dad was built like a Russian weightlifter – stocky and immensely strong."

"How come you're nothing like him then?" says Peter.

"Maybe his mum had an affair with the postman," says Ollie.

"Shut up, Ollie," I say. "Just because I'm getting out of PE."

"Anyway, talking of bodies, what d'you think of Davey?" asks Peter nodding out onto the field where Davey is running around doing his best to avoid the ball.

"He's OK," I say. "Bit of a geek…"

"No, I mean…" Peter lowers his voice. "Well, look at him…"

It's true Davey does seem kinda different. In the wind, his clothes look sort of… empty.

Peter shuffles closer. "Do you think he has image issues?"

"Image issues? Davey?"

"At the party, he hardly ate a thing," says Peter.

"One Dorito," agrees Ollie.

"Well, maybe he wasn't hungry," I say.

Peter shrugs and gets to his feet. "When have you ever known Davey not hungry?"

Tuesday 7th April – Easter holidays!!!!

Yes! Easter break. Kinda typical that I make myself immobile just days before the holidays – I could've probably earned a small fortune gardening for "mum's people" (emphasis on the word "small"). Still, at least you don't need functioning ankles to practise the guitar, which means I have nearly two weeks to work solidly on my "One" Metallica tab. I should do a bit of revision but this is second on my list of priorities. After all, I won't need to know about the chemical reactions of metal carbonates when I'm a hugely rich and successful rock legend!

On a similar note, hair is now long enough to be pulled back into a tiny ponytail. Extremely tiny. It's more a tuft, really, but the potential's there.

Wednesday 8th April

9.40am: Inner Sanctum

F***ing stupid, bitchin' guitar. F***ing dumb song. F***ING F***ING FRUSTRATION! Stupid thick nylon strings, won't f***ing bend, Fingers hurt like hell, probably permanently F***ED. And where the f*** is fret 20?

10.05am

I realise with reluctance that playing "One" by Metallica is impossible on my acoustic guitar. Not just unbelievably, mind-crushingly, finger-breakingly difficult, but impossible. According to page 7 of my tab, "One" by Metallica uses notes on the 20th fret and my poxy kid's guitar only goes up to 18. I could've saved myself a lot of physical and emotional pain if I'd realised that from the off. I open my leather-bound notebook and cross out "Aim number 2: Master the legendary 'One' by Metallica". I will add it back in if and when I achieve aim number 4, i.e. acquire the fabulous and wondrous Jackson.

Thursday 9th April

Ankle: f***ed and sore.
    Fingers: f***ed and sore.
    Mind: f***ed.

10th April – Good Friday

It's Good Friday, according to my Icons of Metal calendar, but so far there's very little good about it. My sister has Clint round and they are monopolising the lounge. Last time I looked, Clint was shoving chocolates into my sister's mouth! Honestly, I wish they would get a room: preferably one in an active war zone.

I would go out, but my ankle still hurts like hell when I walk on it.

Saturday 11th April

7.00pm: The Duck

Unfortunately, I don't get sick pay, so I have to do my shift at the Duck tonight. Mum says it'll be good for me to get out of the house but what she means is that it'll be good for her to have her "me time". I've a good mind to hide all her trashy magazines. Still, it'll be nice to see Michelle and Derek. Well, Michelle anyway.

7.30pm: Duck, stood at sink

My ankle feels awful. Derek and Michelle are sympathetic, but Mrs Barnes just says: "You don't wash up with your ankles, so I expect those plates to be sparkling."

Talk about mercenary. She and my mother must be related.

12th April – Easter Sunday

I receive a three-pack of creme eggs from my sister with one missing. "Sorry," she says, "but I got a bit peckish. Ha ha!"

My mum buys me a small egg, the chocolate of which is about one micron thick. The box is pink and there's a princess on it (I'm not joking).

13th April – Easter Monday

Mum and Nan have had a blazing row. I heard my dad's name mentioned a couple of times. Poor guy, he's been dead 15 years and he's still getting into trouble.

On the bright side, Nan gave me a proper-sized egg.

Tuesday 14th April

4.30pm: lounge

Davey, Peter and Ollie come round. Luckily, Mum is out. She gets weird if I have more than one friend over at once. God knows what she thinks is going to happen; we're hardly going to have an all-male sex romp. If anyone should be worried about that, it's Peter's mum.

4.32pm

Oh my God, why did I think of that!

4.34pm

Anyway, Ollie starts the conversation by asking if anyone fancies anyone. Apparently there's a girl on the cheese counter in Morrison's who's the spitting image of Jessica Alba. Somehow I doubt this, but Ollie is insistent.

"I wouldn't want to go out with Jessica Alba," Peter says. "She's too perfect."

"Also," I remind him, "you're almost certainly gay."

"Ah, maybe that's it," he says.

"Would you go out with Jessica Alba if she was forty?" Ollie asks.

"Depends," I say, "Jennifer Aniston looked good at forty but not everyone ages so well. Take my mum for instance."

"Your mum's not so bad," says Davey.

"Stop right there, Davey!" I say.

"How come she's never re-married?" Davey goes on.

"Maybe because she's super-strict, mean and frigid," I say.

"That'd do it," agrees Ollie.

"Anyway," I say. "Michelle at the pub is the only girl for me." This isn't strictly true, the way I'm feeling these days, I'd go out with Ollie's Labrador if it walked on hind legs and wore a dress but it pays to look like you've got standards.

"I think I'm destined to be single," says Davey. "Girls don't go for fat guys."

"Fat girls do," I tell him.

"You're not fat, Davey," lies Peter. "You're just... height restricted."

"No, I am," says Davey. "I did lose a bit of weight, but then Mum bought a load of chocolate over Easter and I, um ..."

"Stuffed it!" I supply.

Peter shoots me a weird look. "You know, Davey," he says, "if there's something you want to talk about..."

"No, it's OK," says Davey. "Let's see what's on telly."

We spend the next hour watching a programme about people in Australia dating in the dark (a useful strategy for me in the future, possibly) but then Ollie says he has to leave and before long the others are getting up to go too.

At the front door Peter turns to me and says: "You really are an insensitive prick, Josh, do you know that?"

11.00pm

Er, no, Peter, I didn't.

Wednesday 15th April

4.45pm: Inner Sanctum

Mum asks how my ankle is and I make the ridiculous mistake of telling her it's fine.

6.10pm

Mum asks me to put out the recycling, clean out Ozzy's cage, tidy my room, scrape the mud off my trainers, unload the washing machine and get some semi-skimmed milk from the Co-op. My life of leisure is a distant memory.

I get a text from Ollie inviting me round to his place on Friday. Thank God.

Thursday 16th April

4.10am: Inner Sanctum

I've just woken up in a hell of a sweat, having had a terrible nightmare. My dad was desperately trying to tell me something, but before I could make it out, my mum sucked him straight off the sofa with the vacuum cleaner. Jeez, it was really freaky. I may never be able to use our vacuum again.

No great loss.

Friday 17th April

2.30pm: Ollie's Inner Sanctum

"Does it ever worry you that you don't have a girlfriend?" I ask Ollie.

"Not really," says Ollie. "I have something better!" Ollie reaches under his bed and pulls out a NEXT catalogue.

"OK," I say. "How exactly is a...?"

The catalogue falls open at the women's lingerie page.

"Oh," I say. "I see what you mean, but isn't this a bit... Well, a bit sad and perverted?"

"Probably," agrees Ollie, "but when I do get a girlfriend at least I'll know what sort of lingerie to buy her. You gotta keep up with the latest trends and developments. Girls like that."

"True," I say. "That's very true."

"Take these balcony bras," says Ollie. "It says here they offer support for the fuller breast."

"Let's see," I say, but then Ollie's mum knocks on the door and we have to store the catalogue under the duvet.

Saturday 18th April

2.35pm: kitchen

I ask my sister why we don't get the NEXT catalogue.

"Coz Mum and me don't want you perving over the women's lingerie section," she says.

9.00pm: Duck

Derek let me fry some scampi in his deep fat fryer tonight. He said if Mrs Barnes wasn't looking I could eat the odd one. Yes, living the dream at last!

Sunday 19th April

1.30pm: kitchen

I overhear my sister in the lounge telling Mum she needs to get as much practice as possible cutting hair for her new job at Curl Up and Dye. I bolt down my frosted flakes but just as I get up from the table Mum appears and yanks my hair out of my collar while my sister blocks the exit. I am a poor, cornered fox with nowhere to run.

I say to my sister, "If you give me a Justin Bieber cut, I will never speak to you again."

"Promise?" says my sister.

2.20pm

It's not Justin Bieber but it is very short.

Mum walks around me doing an inspection.

"Excellent," she tells my sister. "Very neat and presentable."

Neat and presentable! FML.

Monday 20th April

8.35am: High Street on way to school

I have just heard the worst possible news: Davey has a girlfriend! Jesus, and to think I was starting to feel sorry for him.

Admittedly, she hasn't seen him yet, at least not in the flesh, but she's seen the photo of him on Facebook – the one I helped create – and his status now brags that he's "in a relationship with Tanya".

It's sickening; Davey has less sex appeal than a cowpat. A cowpat from a very ill cow that is swarming with huge bloated flies. I'm really not coping well with this.

The thing is, he's showing off like some puffed-up peacock. You'd think he'd have more tact. We stop at the crossing on the High Street and press the button even though it makes us look like complete saddo ninnies.

"It's natural too, her hair," he's saying. "Not bleached. I think that's better, don't you, natural hair?"

"I guess," I say. I'm not really bothered. Just having hair would be good enough for me.

"And her eyes are the bluest I've ever seen. Bluer than Megan Fox's."

Oh come on, now he's saying she's hotter than Megan Fox!

A bus is approaching at speed and I'm tempted to push him out in front of it.

"You done your Geography homework?" I ask in a desperate attempt to change the subject. "The stuff about Drumlins?"

"Drumlins," mumbles Davey. "I bet Tanya's got great drumlins."

Unfortunately, the bus has now gone and the green man is flashing. I'll have to kill him on the way home.

10.30am: Tower of Terror

I am still reeling from Davey's news. It's official then; every 15-year-old in the country has a girlfriend except me. I'm feeling the pressure more than ever and it's making me impulsive. Gabrielle Evans is handing out some graph paper. Gabby isn't blessed in the looks department; she has very thick glasses and more spots than a Dalmatian with measles, but she does have nice hair and a passable figure, which is the main thing. I manage to accidentally, on purpose touch her hand as she lays down my paper.

Wow! Her stare takes me aback. That is one disgusted stare. You'd have thought I'd just taken out an AK47 and wasted everyone in the classroom. Gabby hates me, that much is obvious. I'll have to set my sights lower.

11.05am: corridor

Alice, can't-remember-her-last-name, is about four foot nothing. I open the door to the English Block, stand to one side to let her through and give her my biggest smile. She mouths a very obvious "f*** you!" back at me, which as chat up lines go, isn't great, but at least we're communicating.

Tuesday 21st April

9.10am: Geography

Becky Calbag nudges me in the back and says, "I like your haircut."

Yeah, yeah, kick a man when he's down, why don't you? Honestly, I don't know how much more of this I can take.

6.30pm: Inner Sanctum

OK, so the obvious way of getting a girlfriend, i.e. being nice has failed. I clearly need to come up with something more... drastic...

7.10pm

DEATH TO ALL BUT METAL

~~Attractive~~ Not bad looking ~~15, 16,~~ 18-year-old male, 6'ish, skinny athletic, blue eyes, nice nose, GSOH, desperately seeks young woman ~~15-17~~ ~~25-30~~ any age to share a good time, see bands, etc. Must have own money - bit skint - sorry :-(Call now for a good time!

Can I possibly send this in to our local paper?

7.20pm

What if someone replies?!!

Wednesday 22nd April

6.00pm: front room

Davey's Facebook wall is covered with posts from Tanya. I haven't read all of them (quite) but most say things like "Miss you" and "Love you" and have millions of "X"s. How can they miss and love each other when they've never even met!

I sort out Davey's Facebook FarmTown and PurrfectPets. Someone has to keep an eye on things.

Thursday 23rd April

6.15pm: kitchen

"Jesus!" announces my sister. "Listen to this lonely hearts ad. Some tw*t has written: "Fairly attractive 18-year-old male, nice nose, no money, guitar guru, call for a good time!" Jeez, what a catch. I bet he's gonna be swamped with offers. NOT!"

'Maybe he didn't have enough money to put more words," I say.

"Huh?"

"Well, the paper charges 25p per word."

"How d'you know?"

"I just...um..."

"OMG. Tell me that isn't you!" exclaims my sister.

"Of course it's not! I'm not 18, am I?"

"No, and your nose isn't that nice either."

"It's not bad!"

"Guitar Guru! It is you!"

that is. So far, she's barged into my Inner Sanctum twice. Once to get my washing (supposedly) and once to ask if I want a cuppa which is an acceptable intrusion, I guess, given my slight addiction to tea.

Jeez, what a pathetic addiction.

Anyway, I put on my favourite Children of Bodom CD to get inspired for a mammoth day-long session and Mum appears with the tea.

'I wish they wouldn't shout like that,' she shouts.

"Pardon?"

"I said, I wish…"

Reluctantly, I turn down Alexi in full throat. "Pardon Mum?"

'I said, I wish they wouldn't shout and growl like that. The music itself is quite nice."

Quite nice?

Mum, I say, please go and put your head under a giant boulder.

I don't really say this. I say, "Well, the growling kind of adds to the overall aggressive feel."

"Don't you find there's enough aggression in real life?" she says, placing the tea smack down on my perfectly pristine and uncreased Children of Bodom limited edition CD sleeve.

Aargh! Mum, please go and insert a wooden spoon up your…

"Thanks," I say.

"Don't let it get cold."

Finally, she leaves and I grab my trusty nylon string and prepare to rock.

"Oh," she says, poking her head back round the door. "Can you pop round and mow Mrs Wilmslow's lawn. Don't expect much payment; the poor dear's virtually penniless."

I put my head in my hands and feel the life force draining out of me. Did Alexi Laiho spend his youth mowing old ladies' lawns? I don't think so.

2.30pm: Mrs Wilmslow's vast estate

Mrs Wilmslow presses a two-pound coin into my palm and gives me a toothless grin. This is what I get for toiling several hours in the midday sun, heaving her antique, totally useless lawn mower up and down her 30-metre-long garden.

"It's a special one," she says. "Brand new. I should keep that."

Well, there ain't exactly much I can buy with it, I feel like saying, but I just smile and nod and smile and back slowly towards the gate.

"You did do the edges, didn't you?" she says.

The edges? OMG! I consider lying but it's clear that the edges have not been done and even though Mrs Wilmslow is about eighty and probably not over endowed in the eyesight department she has noticed my hesitation and is heading hot foot to the shed to get the edging tool or whatever the stupid thing is called.

At midnight I finish the edges. OK, I exaggerate, it's about 3pm but I've still been here more than three hours. I must look a bit hot (as in red, sweaty and suffering heat stroke rather than amazingly attractive) as Mrs Wilmslow offers me some elderflower cordial and a bourbon (biscuit not whiskey). Maybe you'd like to pop back next week, she says.

"Maybe," I say. But then again, maybe I'd rather set fire to my pubes.

On the way home, I console myself by stopping off at Steve's Music Emporium on the High Street. There she is, my beautiful, blue ghost-flamed Jackson. Check out those Seymour Duncan Humbucking Pickups. I go inside to get a closer look.

"One day," I whisper, "you will be mine and I will cradle you in my arms and stroke your slender neck."

A middle-aged women leafing through some flute music gives me a panicky look and hurries away.

"The guitar," I say. "I was talking to the guitar!" But she's gone and is running off up the road.

6.20pm: Duck

"You've caught the sun," says Michelle, loading glasses into the washer.

"I've been working outside," I say.

Michelle smiles and leaves with some clean glasses.

I notice Derek has paused mid-fry and is looking over at me. "You could just ask her out, you know," he says.

"Hmm," I say.

"What's the worst that could happen?" he says.

I say, that she starts gagging and I spend the rest of my life as a sad and emotionally crippled wreck.

Actually, I just shrug and go back to my lettuce.

10.45pm

I can't ask her out. I just can't. It would be like asking Kirk Hammett of Metallica for guitar lessons.

Sunday 26th April

Peter comes round but only stays an hour because he has "to go home and make some important calls". God knows who to. He makes it sound like he's President Obama's personal secretary or something.

I text Davey to find out if he wants to come over but he texts back to say that he's meeting Tanya outside Morrisons. She's coming from Croydon especially to see him. He's planning to take her to Starbucks and buy her a small vanilla latte. "Ciao for now!" he texts.

Well all I can say is I hope she appreciates it. Those vanilla lattes don't come cheap.

No reply from lonely hearts column.

Is that a good or a bad thing?

I don't know!

Monday 27th April

1.10pm: astroturf

"So," says Ollie eagerly. "Did you park your bike in her garage?"

"Pardon?" says Davey.

"Plant your seeds in her garden?"

"Eh?"

"Insert your memory stick in her USB hub?"

"Certainly not!" says Davey. "She's 15, Ollie; it's against the law."

"So is driving a tractor but you'd sure as hell do it if no one was watching, wouldn't you?" says Ollie.

"Actually, she couldn't come," says Davey. "Her mum wouldn't let her."

"Mums!" I say.

"You could go to her house instead!" announces Peter as if he's just cracked some top-secret code.

"Mum won't let me."

"Mums!" I say.

"My dad's best mate used to drive a tractor," says Ollie.

Thankfully, the bell goes then and we all troop inside. I can't wait to go to college and make some new friends; the ones I have are mentally subnormal.

Tuesday 28th April

8.30am: kitchen

We can't find Ozzy!

Sure, he's always escaping from his cage but usually I can find him somewhere contentedly gnawing holes in things. Not today though; I searched everywhere. And worse still, I've just noticed that my top window is open!

I am so worried I can barely get ready for school. In fact, I shouldn't be going to school; I should be roaming the streets rattling bags of Ferret Feast, knocking on doors and breaking into people's sheds. But Mum insists that I go. I have 100 percent attendance and if I keep this up the school will pay for me to go to the Year 11 Prom, thus saving Mum about thirty rotten quid. Basically, if I were in the advanced stages of pneumonia she'd stuff a cough sweet in my gob and boot me out the door.

9.20am: Maths

It's impossible to concentrate. I'm supposed to be solving linear equations of the form $ax + b = cx + d$ but I just can't get into it.

11.30am: English

Mrs Barber tells me I have a chance of getting an A on the language paper if I don't overdo the analogies. I don't know what she's talking about. I'm about as likely to overdo the analogies as some dumb chavette who wouldn't spot an analogy if it jumped out of her bargain bucket of chicken and landed on her Burberry-check shell suit. Mrs Barber then informs the class that for maximum effect our essays should have strong narrative thrust, which sets all the immature saddos off into fits of giggles. I feel ashamed of myself laughing so much when poor Ozzy is missing.

During break, Ollie mentions that his History teacher said a sandwich was the cause of the Titanic sinking.

"Do you learn anything not sandwich-related in History?" I ask him.

Ollie shrugs. "Don't you want to know how it did it?" he says.

"No," I say, "but I do have an excellent sandwich-related joke. A sandwich walks into a bar and the barman says: "Sorry mate, we don't serve food!"

"Shut up, Josh," says Peter. "I'd like to know, Ollie."

"Well, the captain was a bit peckish and decided to grab a quick bite…"

I close my ears and try to slip into a metal-stardom daydream. All Ollie's sandwich stories are remarkably similar.

3.45pm

On the way home I text Mum to see if Ozzy has been found. I have already secretly texted her in Maths, English and Additional Science. She was not amused but this is what she gets for making me go to school. Anyway, it turns out that Ozzy is still missing so I must now do what I should have done eight hours ago.

The first door I knock on belongs to old Mr Marshall, sadly in no way related to the manufacturers of Marshall amps. Mr Marshall comes to the door in his tartan slippers and baggy brown trousers. He stinks of lavender for some reason but I put this to the back of my mind.

"Um, hi Mr Marshall," I say. "I don't suppose you've seen Ozzy on your travels."

"Ozzy?"

"Ozzy, my ferret. He's gone missing."

"Have you looked down yer trousers?" says Mr Marshall.

"Pardon?" I say.

"Down yer trousers, lad! That's where he'll be."

"Um, sorry, what?"

Mr Marshall leans closer. "I always keep a ferret down me trousers. You never know when you're gonna get lucky!"

I'm not sure if Mr Marshall is senile, perverted or just has a very warped sense of humour. Maybe the constant reek of lavender has mutated his brain. Anyway, he's about as much use as a condom made of bubble wrap so I go to the next house along.

And the next.

And the next.

No one has seen Ozzy.

Wednesday 29th April

7.15pm: Inner Sanctum

My sister comes in and tells me to shut my eyes and hold out my hands.

Something soft and furry is laid on my palms. I squint down and start screaming. It is Ozzy and he is dead! "Oh my God, how could you?" I say. "Oh my God!!"

"For f*** sake!" yells my sister. "It's a wig!"

I look down properly and see that it is indeed a wig; a long, black silky one.

"We were having a clear-out at Curl Up and Dye," says my sister. "I thought you could practice headbanging in it. Jesus, you have a very girly scream, d'you know that?"

"Oh, um, thanks," I say. "Um..."

My sister shrugs and leaves. Practice headbanging? How sad does she think I am?

8.00pm

It has only taken me 45 minutes to learn to whirl my wig in perfect time to "Ride the Lightning" by Metallica. Clearly, I'm a natural. If only Mum would let me grow my hair. Girls would be falling over themselves to stroke my lustrous locks.

Locks so long, the girls will tumble

Into my arms for a quick fumble

Thursday 30th April

5.40pm: Inner Sanctum

Davey has invited me round his house after school to do some revision. He says we can learn together, but what will actually happen is that I'll spend two hours trying to show him how to do quadratic equations and failing because Davey is about as talented at maths as sheep are at pole vaulting. I decide to go anyway, since Mum has been nagging me to clean my room (again!) and remove the poster of Alice Cooper getting his head sawn off. I keep telling her it's not real, but she thinks I'm developing sadistic tendencies. Also, Davey has high-speed internet access with no parental control and Xbox controllers that glow in the dark.

7.15pm: Davey's not-so-humble abode

Davey looks a bit put out when I arrive.

"Wassup?" I say.

"Tanya's dumped me," he says. "She said I might be a forty-year-old paedophile. She says she can't take the risk."

"That's crazy," I say. "She must've seen your picture... Oh, wait..."

"Exactly," says Davey.

Well, I have mixed feelings. I must admit part of me is glad, but Davey looks so downhearted I also feel guilty.

"Don't worry," I say. "There's plenty more fish in the sea."

"But I don't want a fish," Davey says. He really did say that and he wasn't even trying to be funny.

"I mean there'll be other girls," I say. "And anyway I've been thinking about all this and I'm wondering if we're a bit too young to be worried about girls. You know, Davey, there are actually loads of boys who haven't got girlfriends at our school. And even the ones who have don't really go out with them. They just hang around school and maybe outside Morrisons. What sort of relationship is that? I think we've been fooled into submitting to peer pressure and we should just stop and say no! No, I will not feel inferior. I refuse to feel like a loser just because some bimbo isn't trying to lick my tonsils... And besides, a girl will come along in her own good time. Probably when we're least expecting it!"

Davey is looking at me oddly. "Can we do some revision now?" he says.

We revise for about twenty minutes (there's only so much you can take of quadratic equations), then go on YouTube for a bit. We spend 45 minutes looking at people having dramatic mobility scooter accidents, ferrets playing the piano (where are you, Ozzy?) and some girl giving a tutorial on how to have anime hair. She's quite nice looking so we watch that a few times and pause it occasionally.

Then it's back to maths for a few minutes before firing up the Xbox. Davey throws me a plastic guitar and I spend the next hour attempting to press coloured buttons in the right order while trying not to listen to "Number One Hits of the Eighties".

Davey thrashes me good and proper on the guitar game but I can't say I'm bothered. It's nothing like playing a real guitar, not even a crappy little nylon string for eight-year-olds. Besides which, I kinda let him win on account of feeling sorry for him.

Friday 1st May

7.45am: Inner Sanctum

I flip over the page of my Icons of Metal calendar to see the face of Ozzy Osbourne leering at me. My Ozzy has now been missing for four days. I am trying to come to terms with the fact that I may never see him again, but it's very hard. "It's OK for you," I say to the human Ozzy. "You probably never had a beloved pet who was the only one who would listen to all your teenage traumas." I give my eyes a good rub on my sleeve; the hayfever's been really bad these last few days.

I can't be sure, but I feel that Ozzy's leer is an understanding one. Personally, I don't believe he ever did those mean things to bats and I know for a fact that Sharon likes dogs so I'm thinking

Ozzy would probably be sympathetic. Anyway, regardless of Ozzy's feelings on the matter, life must go on. Unfortunately.

Saturday 2nd May

9.00am: Inner Sanctum

We're into May and soon it'll be exam time. I have made a revision timetable, but I have not spent hours on it like Peter, colour coding it, cross-hatching areas and adding "cool" drop-shadow effects. If Peter spent half the time he did making his timetable on revising, he might actually pass something.

Amazingly, Mum suggested I stop doing jobs for "her people" and working at The Duck Revived until my exams are over. She said if I revise hard, I might get a well-paid job and be able to keep her in a life of luxury in her old age. Er, yes Mum, whatever you say. Actually, I've decided to keep working (and earning) as long as possible. As I told her, it's perfectly possible to mow lawns, walk dogs, wash up and revise at the same time.

6.20pm: bathroom

"Will you get out of the bathroom," yells my sister banging on the door. "What the hell are you doing in there? No, don't answer that!"

I have been in the bathroom precisely eighteen minutes. Admittedly, it usually takes me about three to get ready for the Duck but I have a few face craters that I don't want Michelle seeing.

"Josh, I am meeting Clint in one hour and thirty-five minutes and I haven't got any make-up on or even straightened my hair so please will you F * * * ING HURRY UP!"

I open the door while she is still yelling. "All yours," I say. "And you really shouldn't spit in people's faces. It's not very ladylike."

She yells something even less ladylike but I am downstairs and out the door so I can pretend I didn't hear. Ha!

7.25pm: Duck

I'm on washing-up duty again at the Duck. Yay! This is what it's about. Why would I want to be partying or moshing at some wild metal gig when I can be here scraping the grease off several thousand plates? At least I have brought my phone with me so I can have some decent music to drown out the yodelling vocals on the radio.

Mrs Barnes comes in and tells me I should stop making salad garni and go help Michelle as it is crazy busy and she is struggling to get the orders out. "Take these tuna paninis to table 12 will you?" she says, passing me a tray. "Hurry now; they congeal if they're left too long."

I head out into the pub and am just about to round the corner to table 12 when I hear something familiar and horrible, i.e. Clint's voice. Jeez, why did he bring my sister to this dump? I hope she won't expect a staff discount. Mrs Barnes doesn't believe in them, at least not for lowly washer-uppers like me.

Shit!

I dart back behind a handy beam. It is Clint but he's not with my sister. He's with some other girl! A very attractive girl, actually, and he's got his arm round her.

Luckily, The Duck Revived has lots of nooks and crannies, so I creep round to get a better view through some vases of dead wheat and stuff.

"What are you doing?" says Michelle, who has suddenly appeared beside me.

"Oh, hi," I whisper. "I'm watching that boy and girl over there make out."

"OMG! You pervert!"

"No, no," I hiss. "That's my sister's boyfriend. She was s'posed to be seeing him tonight but look, he's with this other girl."

"Oh," says Michelle, inching one of the vases aside to get a better look. "Oh, the bastard. Urgh, he's practically eating her face off."

"I know," I say. "There's no way I can give them these paninis."

Michelle nods. "I'll do it," she says.

"Thanks," I say. "You're a lifesaver."

I creep back to the kitchen and try to think what to do but I can't get my head straight. Maybe I should text Ollie. He always knows what to do in situations like these. What am I talking about? He won't have a clue what to do. I text him anyway:

Clint sposed 2 b with Maddie but with other girl. Should I tell her?

Ollie texts back: **Who is Clint?**

Me: **Maddies bfriend.**

Ollie: **Who is Maddie?**

I sometimes wonder if Ollie is annoying on purpose. Surely no one could be that useless without trying. Plus, I now have soap all over my phone and Mrs Barnes has appeared at the doorway.

"I have just had a complaint from table 12," she says. "Those paninis were stone cold. I thought I told you to deliver them straight away."

"Sorry," I say. "I got distracted."

"So I see," she says with a voice that could dice cucumber. "Derek? Put these in the microwave please and this time, Joshua, get them out immediately."

"OK," I say.

"I shall be watching and I want to see you go and apologise."

"Apologise? Never," I blurt out.

"I beg your pardon!"

"It's just…"

"You will go and apologise, Joshua, or you will hand in your apron!"

"Hand in my apron?"

Derek passes me the paninis. "Get sacked, mate," he explains.

"Oh," I say.

Mrs Barnes puts her hands on her hips.

"Fine," I say wearily.

"Tell him he's a shitface," whispers Michelle as I leave.

Just as I get to table 12, I look round and see that it's so busy at the bar that Mrs Barnes has had to serve. I put the paninis down on the edge of the table and turn double-quick. No way am I apologising to that idiot!

Clint and the good-looking girl are totally engrossed with each other and barely even register my existence, so it's a mystery why I then go and do something really, really stupid…

"Why aren't you with my sister?" I say, turning back.

"Jesus," says Clint. "What the f*** are you doing here?"

"I work here," I say.

"F*** me."

"Why aren't you with my sister?" I say again. "She's got all done up and straightened her hair and everything."

"What's he talking about, Clint?" says the good-looking girl.

"Nothing," says Clint. "I chucked his cheatin' bitch of a sister last week."

"What?" I say. "My sister wouldn't cheat!"

Clint folds his arms and sits back in his chair. "The women in your family ain't as innocent as you think, mate," he says.

"Huh?" I say. "What d'you mean?"

"Is everything OK here?" asks Mrs Barnes materialising behind me like a magician's assistant.

"Fine," says Clint. "Everything's fine."

Mrs Barnes glares at me and leaves, but as soon as she's gone, Clint gets up, twists my arm behind my back and frog-marches me behind the wheat sheaves.

"Listen, dork breath," he hisses. "If you breathe a word of this to your sister I'll f***ing smash that stupid little guitar of yours and ram it so far up yer arse you'll be burping arpeggios. Got it?"

"Got it," I say.

10.45pm: lounge

When I get home my sister is looking sadder than a Labrador puppy that's lost its toilet roll.

"Hair looks nice," I say. "Very, um, straight."

Mum gives me a WTF look and orders me to put the kettle

on. I am tempted to say, excuse me but I've been on my feet for the last four hours up to my arms in leftover paninis! But I can be sensitive to atmospheres, so I do as I'm told.

11.30pm: lying in bed

Should I tell my sister or not?

Would it hurt her feelings too much?

Would she even believe me?

And how does Clint know what arpeggios are?

Sunday 3rd May

9.50am: kitchen

I've decided to keep quiet on the Clint front largely because if Clint destroys my guitar I will have to practise on a Tupperware container with elastic bands wrapped round it and I know from experience that elastic bands are impossible to tune.

Anyway, I'm expecting Maddie to be in a bad mood, partly due to last night and partly because, well, why break the habit of a lifetime? However, it seems she has broken it because she is surprisingly chirpy.

"Want some tea?" she chirps. "I'm making a pot."

"You're offering me a cup of tea?" I say.

"Yes, dear brother and don't act so suspicious. It makes your eyes go snidey."

"Thanks," I say. "For the tea, that is. So you, um, seem a lot happier."

She points towards some flowers on the window sill. "Clint

delivered them first thing. Lovely, aren't they?"

"Very nice," I manage.

"His mum was taken ill last night and he had to take her to the hospital. It was such a worry he forgot to text. Seems that she's OK though."

"Ah," I say as she puts down the teapot.

"Poor Clint. He was so apologetic. There were actual tears in his eyes. He's such a big softie..."

I start to feel a bit nauseous but thankfully someone knocks at the front door so I can escape before she gushes on.

"Hey!" I say. "Ollie, my man! To what do I owe..."

"I get it," he says.

"What?"

"Your text."

"Oh," I say. "Oh, don't worry about that. That's all forgotten now. Want a drink?"

Ollie follows me into the kitchen.

"Yes," he goes on relentlessly. "You meant Maddie your sister. You meant Clint was with another girl and not your sister!"

"What?" says Maddie.

"Oh hi," says Ollie. "Didn't, er, see you there."

"Um," I say backing towards the hall. "I've got this difficult problem in Stratified Sampling. Can you just come up..."

"Stay here, Ollie!" roars my sister. "What was that you said about Clint?"

Ollie swallows. He looks at me the same way Ozzy used to when I took him to the vet. (Poor Ozzy.)

I shake my head subtly but I am crap at being subtle and

Maddie gives me a murderous glare.

"Stop that, Josh," she snaps, "unless you want to see what scalding hot tea does to your balls. Go on, Ollie."

"Well, um..."

I couldn't inflict such cruelty on my worst enemy let alone a reasonably good mate, so I decide to tell her everything. "Clint was in the Duck last night," I say. "He was with this girl. They seemed quite... close."

"You're lying," she snaps.

"Scouts honour," I say, making the little scout symbol and putting on a goofy smile.

Ollie grins but Maddie doesn't see the funny side.

"You and Mum have always hated Clint and now you're trying to split us up!" she cries.

God, and I thought I was delusional. But then she takes a deep, shuddery breath and stares down at the table. "What did she look like then? This girl. Was she... pretty?"

"I don't know," I lie. "She was fairly pretty, I guess. If you like that sort of thing. She had dark hair and blue eyes. She left an order for two paninis at the bar under the name of Katie Price."

"What? Jordan?" says Ollie. "Jeez, the lucky bastard."

"Shut up, Ollie," I say. "It wasn't Jordan."

"You sure? Did you get a look at her boobs?"

"It wasn't Jordan!"

My sister keeps staring at the sugar bowl.

"Sorry, sis," I say, "but you're way too good for Clint. He's a serious jerk-off. Plus you're not unattractive." (It's true that she inherited all the good-looking genes.) "You'll soon find another boyfriend…" but she has got up and left the room.

"God, imagine if Jordan lived here," says Ollie dreamily. "We could be stood next to her at the fish counter in Sainsbury's. She could be sunbathing in the park, topless!"

12.15pm: Transept to Forbidding Portal

Finally Ollie has gone. Thank God. Some people don't half go on about their fantasies.

Behind me I can hear harsh words being spoken on the phone. "Screw you, you limp-dicked ****hole!" screams my sister before slamming down the receiver. My sister is never one to hold back on the insults.

"Bastard's chucked," she tells me.

I nod my approval. "You know, he said something really weird in the pub," I say. He said, 'The women in your family aren't all that innocent, you know.' What's he mean by that?"

"I have no idea," says my sister. "Maybe Gran used to be a pole dancer or something."

Hmm, thanks for that, sis.

12.30pm: Inner Sanctum

Davey has just popped round to give me some "Missing Ferret" posters he's made. Davey's dad works at a place where there are free photocopying facilities, or at least they're free if you do it after everyone else has gone home. The posters are very good if you ignore the fact that Davey's drawing of Ozzy makes him look like an overweight squirrel. Who's gonna worry about a

I leave my sister wiping tears of hilarity from her eyes. Nice to know my nightmare of an existence brings happiness to others.

Friday 24th April

4.50pm: park

Mr Pitman is having a good day with his arthritis today, so I push him down to the park (in his wheelchair, that is!) and he buys me a Strawberry Mivi ice lolly and Minty a Mini Milk. It's a bit cold for ice creams but I don't want to hurt his feelings by saying no.

Anyway, for some reason I find myself telling Mr Pitman all about my lack of success in the "girlfriend" department. "No one fancies me," I say slurping my lolly miserably. "And apparently my nose isn't that nice."

I am being pathetic but Mr Pitman kindly doesn't point that out. "Your nose is fine," he says. "And you are still very young, Josh. At your age, I was playing football and listening to music. Don't let peer pressure get to you; a girl will come along in her own good time. Probably when you least expect it."

"Yeah," I say. I feel better after talking to Mr Pitman. I bend down to give Minty a friendly pat but she hasn't yet finished her Mini Milk and so growls at me savagely.

Saturday 25th April

8.45am: Inner Sanctum

It's Saturday! Hooray. With any luck I should be able to get in eight hours of guitar practice today. If Mum'll leave me alone, missing squirrel, for heaven's sake? Still, the thought was there.

I have a quick lunch of smoky bacon crisps and frosted cornflakes before going out and sticking up Davey's posters. I have underlined the word "FERRET" several times and promised a reward of all my PlayStation 2 games. Some of them may be antiques but Ozzy must come first and, besides, I haven't got anything else worth having.

11.55pm: Inner Sanctum

I am finding it hard to sleep. It's hot and my mind is brimming over with irregular verbs and the odd illicit thought of Michelle. It's a shame we don't do sex education for GCSE. I reckon I'd be great at the practicals!

Actually, I'd be crap.

Anyway, I really must get some sleep...

Huh? What was that?

I sit bolt upright convinced that I hear something down the corridor. I keep perfectly still, listening, but there's nothing. Guess I must've been ...

Shit, there it is again! It sounds like someone trying to break in.

Oh God, who is it? What is it?

I sit very still, sweating like onions in a wok. Being the man of the house, I suppose I should go and investigate. There again, Maddie's right hook is way better than mine and her nails are like daggers.

Just as I'm about to get up, Maddie appears in the doorway in her Hello Kitty nightdress. Her face is even whiter than Kitty's.

She creeps in and sits on the edge of the bed. Unfortunately, it's just us in the house tonight; Mum has gone to stay with Aunt Sarah in Reading who has given birth to twins. Yes, Mum feels that a woman in her mid-thirties is more in need of help than her own defenceless children. God, I wish Dad was here. He'd sort out any burglars.

"What is it?" Maddie whispers.

I shrug helplessly. "Have you got your phone?" I say.

"Downstairs. Yours?"

"Out of battery."

"Well, that's a lot of good, isn't it!" she hisses.

"At least I didn't leave it downstairs!"

"At least I remembered to CHARGE MINE UP!"

"Sssh!" I hiss.

We are at an impasse but then I realise the noise has stopped. "OK," I say. "Go downstairs and get your phone. If anything else happens we'll call the police."

"I'm not going down!" she exclaims. "Josh, you really are the most self-centred..."

I could say, well at least I'm not a two-timing, slimy, backstabbing w***er. But it's probably not the best time to bring Clint up. God, what if it is Clint, trying to force his way in? If it is, I'm dead.

"OK. Fine," I say, "but if I get killed, promise you won't read the leather-bound notebook Mum got me. It's got some lyrics I was experimenting with in and, um, other stuff."

"I promise."

"I want the Children of Bodom song, 'Better off Dead' played at my funeral and I want to be cremated, otherwise I might wake up in the coffin and you know how claustrophobic I get. I want Davey to have my collection of oddly shaped tortilla chips and Ollie that CD we did of us farting to Britney's 'Oops I did it again'. ."

"You're stalling for time," she says. "Get going."

I sigh and start making my way down the corridor. I have just got past the bathroom when suddenly there's a loud thud. It's coming from Mum's bedroom!

Jesus, this is scary. There's the sound of repeated knocking and then an even louder thud. My sister has crept up behind me holding something black and shiny. I peer closer. "Straighteners? You think they'll want their hair done?"

She makes a face and gives me the finger.

I open Mum's door and reach for the light. "OK," I say. "Game's up. And don't try any funny business 'cause my sister's armed!"

"Dook dook," says Ozzy.

Monday 4th May

12.20am: Mum's bedroom

So our mystery burglar/murderer/poltergeist turns out to be none other than our long-lost Ozzy! It looks like he'd squeezed into the bottom drawer of Mum's wardrobe, ate half a woollen blanket, and then couldn't squeeze back out again, at least not without a mammoth effort. I'm actually quite proud of him.

While my sister takes super-sized Ozzy back to my room, I

get a dustpan and brush and start cleaning out the drawer. There are ferret droppings and pieces of wool everywhere. I am just sweeping up the bits when I spot what looks like the corner of a book poking out from under an old jumper.

Wow, it's a leather-bound notebook! Just like the one Mum gave me, only much older. I open the cover and see the words: STRICTLY PRIVATE – DO NOT READ!

I dive into the middle of the book.

There's some photos of Mum at a club with this eighties-looking band playing. Check out those poodle perms! I skip ahead.

23rd Dec: Yet another lonely Christmas looms. I may as well not be married.

Hmm, bit depressing. I skip ahead again.

4th June: One month to go before my life changes forever! Can't keep this secret any longer, it's tearing me apart…

Secret? Hey, this is getting interesting! I turn the page eagerly but suddenly I come over a bit weird. I can't help remembering how bad it felt when I caught Ollie reading my secret diary. I feel guilty, excited and kinda sick at the same time. Should I read or not. To read or not to…

Oh, it's no good, I can't do it. I close the book and shove it back in the drawer under the jumper. I bundle up the chewed blanket, run downstairs and stuff it in the bin bag outside. That book was written ages ago; if Mum did have any secrets, well, they can't be anything to do with me.

12.40am: Inner Sanctum

"Manage to clean up OK?" says Maddie, poking her head round my door.

"Yep," I say.

"Cool. Well, good night."

"Night," I say. "Er, Maddie, you know Mum?"

"Our mum?"

"She hasn't told you any, like, interesting secrets has she?"

"Huh?" she says.

"Oh, nothing," I say.

My sister shakes her head. "Well, see you in the morning."

"Right," I say".

When I finally get into bed, I can hear Ozzy jumping about and chattering away in his cage. I lift him out and sit on the bed to give him a cuddle but immediately he darts away and starts leaping around under the duvet.

It's a terrible thing to say but for a few seconds I almost wish he were still missing.

Tuesday 5th May

3.50pm: school

It's just me and Davey walking home tonight, as Ollie has a dental appointment. Davey is propping up the wall outside the gym and has the same expression you see on men waiting outside women's changing rooms, i.e. verging on suicidal.

"Wassup?" I say to Davey.

Davey shrugs, "Not much."

We wander on a bit in silence.

"PE tomorrow," I say. "D'you think Mr Cox will make us do squat thrusts again? My legs hurt for a week after that."

"At least you could do some," says Davey. "I barely got off the ground."

"Ha!" I say.

More silent wandering.

"Oh well, like when you ever gonna need to do squat thrusts in real life?" I say.

"I s'pose," says Davey.

"Unless you wanna join the army!"

"Not really," says Davey. "Think I might try and be a quantity surveyor."

"That sounds... great," I say.

We've arrived at Davey's place now.

"Well, see you tomorrow then," I say.

Davey suddenly turns to me and says, "Josh, are you happy?"

"Eh?" I say. "Well, I guess so. Aren't you?"

"Not really."

I want to ask Davey why, but he has turned his back and is halfway up his drive.

4.30pm

Happy? Happy? What sort of a question is that?

7.00pm: kitchen

Over tea (decent fish fingers, for once, with no black bits) I say, "Mum, I think Davey's having a mid-teen crisis. He says he's not happy."

"What?" says my mum. "Well, he jolly well ought to be; he's got his whole life ahead of him."

"Yeah," chimes in my sister, "a whole life of misery."

"Rubbish," says my mum. "These are the best..."

"Stop, Mum," I say. "Please don't say that."

"Anyway," she goes on. "Wait till he gets to my age, then he'll have something to worry about. I mean, what's left for an old has-been like me?"

"Oh well..."

"There are days when I wish I wouldn't wake up."

"Oh well..."

"Days when I wish I could sleep forever."

"Mum!" I say. "Don't be silly. You're not that old."

"Well, I feel it," she says. "And believe me, there are no advantages to getting old, Josh."

"Ha," I say. "You're wrong there; you don't have to put up with that high-pitched noise outside Morrison's for a start."

"I would love to hear it," says Mum.

Wednesday 6th May – less than 2 months till my 16th birthday

6.00pm: park with Mr Pitman and Minty

This whole happiness thing has been weighing on my mind. I ask Mr Pitman if he is happy and, amazingly, he says yes! He says he has some good friends (not just Mum and me!) who come over to share a few beers and that he enjoys the simple things in life, such as curries and listening to music.

I ask what sort of music he likes, expecting him to go on about some classical crap, but it turns out Mr Pitman is a big fan of AC/DC!

"I can play some AC/DC on my guitar," I tell him.

"Excellent," says Mr Pitman. "I used to dabble on the guitar, too."

"Really?" I say, and I must sound a bit surprised 'cause Mr Pitman says, "You can't always judge an album by its cover, Josh."

Mr Pitman is dead right there. When I saw the cover for Anthrax's, Fistful of Metal album I thought the music was gonna be totally lacking in pace and lyrical development whereas, in fact, it was neither of those things.

Thursday 7th May

7.15pm: Scouts

Hmm, I still can't get what Davey said out of my head. I'm supposed to be showing some younger scouts how to tie a midshipman's hitch but I'm finding it hard to summon up the enthusiasm.

10.00pm: Inner Sanctum

Ozzy scrambles onto my bed, rolls around and starts making dooking noises. He is very easily pleased.

The trouble is most people aren't like ferrets; they think about stuff too much, put too many pressures on themselves and get upset and disappointed when things don't work out. All of which reminds me to look over the goals in my notebook.

11.01pm

FML!

Friday 8th May

8.50am

On the way into school Davey hurries up to me, looking worried.

"Davey," I say. "Please don't ask me if I'm happy or if there's any point to life 'cause I'm kinda afraid of what my answer might be."

"Eh?" says Davey. "I was gonna ask if you've done the RE homework."

"Oh," I say. "Damn!"

2.30pm: RE

I tell Mrs Higginbotham that as a committed atheist (98 percent sure of God's non-existence) I refuse to revise RE or do any RE related homework on conscientious objector grounds.

Mrs Higginbotham says, "OK, fine."

You'd think she'd try to convince me otherwise. I mean it's

not like it matters to me how many GCSEs I get.

Wait...

6.45pm: kitchen

On the way home, Davey told me that his mum has promised him £25 for every A or A-star he gets. It's a fairly safe bet, since Davey is unlikely to get even one. I, on the other hand, could be looking at two, or even three! I decide to bring the subject up with Mum over tea.

"Mum, I'm not sure there's much point revising that hard," I say between mouthfuls of tinned spaghetti. "I mean, who really cares if I get good grades?"

Mum stops washing up and looks at me. "I do," she says.

"Really? It means a lot to you then, me doing well?"

"Absolutely."

"Does it mean, say, £30?"

"Pardon?"

"Well, Davey's mum..."

I plough on, expecting a lecture any second, but Mum just nods and listens and nods some more. Not once does she butt in with the Financial Difficulties stuff.

"So, um, what d'you think?" I say.

"Absolutely," she agrees. "You're growing up so fast, Josh. I can't treat you as a kid any longer. There are things you should... Things I ought...."

"What's up, Mum?" I say.

"Nothing," she says and she grabs her bag from the back of the chair and takes out her cheque book. "Here's some money in advance. Seeing as I know you're going to do really well."

Money in advance! WTF?

"£100," she says, ripping off a cheque. "Put it towards that guitar you're always on about."

I am so shocked that I forget to close my mouth and a huge dollop of spaghetti falls into my lap.

7.20pm: Inner Sanctum

I empty the contents of the pickle jar on my bed and start counting. With the cheque it comes to £380.32! Wow, just over £100 to go. I may actually be able to do it!

Saturday 9th May

10.35am: kitchen

"On, by the way," says my sister, passing me a school book, "this girl came round while you were in the shower. Said you left this in class."

"What girl?" I say.

"She didn't say her name but she had kind of…" My sister makes weird circular motions with her hands.

'What?" I say. "She had kind of what?

"You know." Circular motions again.

'Don't keep doing that," I say irritably. "What did she have?"

"MASSIVE TITS!" yells my sister.

"Oh," I say. "That must've been Becky Calbag. She sits behind me in Geography."

"That was nice of her, bringing your work over," says Mum coming into the kitchen.

"Yeah," I say. "Amazingly nice seeing as she hates my guts."

"Josh," tsks Mum. "Sometimes I think you're paranoid."

"I am not!" I say. "Just 'cause everyone hates me does not mean I'm paranoid!"

8.00pm: Duck kitchen

"How's your sister?" says Michelle.

"Oh, her usual horrible, psychotic self," I say.

Michelle rolls her eyes. "I mean, did you tell her about her boyfriend?"

"Oh," I say. "Yeah, I kinda had to. Anyway, she's chucked him."

"Good for her," says Michelle. "And by the way, that was very brave of you last week, standing up to him. I was well impressed."

"Oh, um..." I say. "Really? Well, er. Um..." My face goes redder than a sunburnt lobster but luckily Michelle has gone back to the bar.

"You're in there!" says Derek, giving me a wink.

"Nah," I say.

"Ask her out," he urges.

"Shh, Derek. I can't," I say.

"Why not?"

"I don't fancy her."

"F*** off," scoffs Derek.

"I don't!" I say.

"You're too chicken. That's what it is. I should cut you up into little bits, cover you in batter and chuck you into this 'ere fryer!"

I used to really like Derek but I've gone off him a bit now.

10.10pm: Inner Sanctum

Oh God, Derek is right; I am a chicken and what's more, if Kirk Hammett walked into my room, I would ask him for a lesson. Of course I would!

So OK, I'll ask her out. But I have to do it right. I'll have to learn some really good chat-up lines. Something that'll knock her off her feet. Metaphorically speaking.

Sunday 10th May

10.45am: front room

I'm copying potential chat-up lines from the internet into my leather-bound notebook. So far I have:

Is it hot in here or is it just you? This would work well in the Duck as it's usually bloody boiling, especially in the kitchen.

I lost my phone number. Can I have yours? Naff, but quite funny.

You're so hot that when I look at you I get a tan. Just naff.

Plus one Ollie texted earlier:

Is that a ladder in your tights or a stairway to heaven? Which pretty much explains why Ollie will never find love – at least not with a girl!

Monday 11th May

3.10pm: La Bastille

There are only five more lessons of French to go, ever! Realising this has put me in an excellent mood, but Madam Zizi won't let that last long.

"Josh," she says. "Qu'est-ce que tu bois d'habitude à midi?"

I think for a while before saying, "J'habite dans une maison?" which has everyone in the class in hysterics, or at least the swotty ones. Most, like me, haven't understood either the question or my answer.

"I didn't ask where you live, Josh," says Madam Zizi with a condescending smile. "I asked what you drank at lunchtime."

"Oh," I say. "Coke."

"In French, Josh."

"Le Coke?"

Madam Zizi grins triumphantly. Yet again, she has made me look "tray stewpeed". I should be left alone for the rest of the lesson now though, so I go back to the list I've been writing: "Things I've got going for me".

It's a bit sad, I know, but it's supposed to be very life-affirming and I need all the affirming I can get right now.

So far I have:

Good at guitar

Kind to animals

Decent nose

Is that it? God, even I wouldn't go out with me.

Ollie kicks my shin and points to a note he's written in the back of his book:

wanna come round after school and revise? Got new zombie game, Brain splatter 2. It's epic.

6.10pm: Ollie's Inner Sanctum

Brain Splatter 2 is epic!

10.10pm: still in Ollie's Inner Sanctum

Disgustingly epic!

11.00pm: my Inner Sanctum

How are kids s'posed to revise when there are all these distractions in the home? I blame the parents.

Tuesday 12th May

8.35am: on the way to school

Davey is seeing a counsellor! She told him to start making a journal of his feelings, so his mum has bought him a large leather-bound notebook.

"Cool," I say. "It'll be like a release valve."

"That's what my counsellor said!" exclaims Davey.

Jesus, I hope Davey's counsellor isn't my mum in disguise!

Wednesday 13th May

8.00pm: front room

I spend the evening revising simultaneous equations and chat-up lines. I hope I don't get them mixed up!

Question 1: What is the difference between the focus and the epicentre of an earthquake?

Answer: Wow, your dad must've been a baker because you've got great buns!

Thursday 14th May

7.30pm: Scouts

We're making animals out of fruit this evening. I got the wrong idea and brought a tin of peaches, but Peter has kindly let me share his mangosteen.

"What shall we use for eyes?" I say.

"Whatever you like," Peter says.

"Well, you must have some ideas," I say.

"I have bigger concerns," says Peter.

"OK," I say. "Let's try these olives..."

"I owe a gay chat line £307.50," says Peter suddenly. "And if I don't pay in ten days, I'm going to court."

"What!"

"My dad will kill me. He doesn't even know I'm almost certainly gay!"

"God," I say. "Well, um, don't you have any savings?"

Peter looks down and shakes his head.

I slice the olives into rings and stick two on the mangosteen.

"I'm going to prison," wails Peter, tears spilling onto his cheeks. "Juvenile detention centre. They'll make me do terrible things like bricklaying and mechanics!"

"No, look, I'll give you the money," I say.

"Really? Oh God, thanks Josh. Thank you. I'll pay you back."

"Yeah, well, I meant I'll lend you the money," I say.

"It may take a while, what with university tuition fees..."

Great...

10.10pm: Inner Sanctum

I take £307.50 from my precious Guitar Fund and stuff it in my pencil case for Peter. I am not a wuss so I don't cry but it's a close run thing. Peter better not call me an insensitive prick again, that's all I can say.

Saturday 16th May

5.00pm: lounge

My sister says Curl Up and Dye are diversifying. They will soon be offering eyebrow tinting, facials and waxing.

"What about piercing?" I say, remembering number 5 on my list of things to achieve.

"Probably," she says, "but I'm not sure I'll be working there much longer."

"Why not?" I say.

My sister shudders. "Because I have to start doing people's back, sack, and crack."

7.00pm: Duck

Michelle is on leave, which is actually a bit of a relief as I still haven't decided which chat-up line to use. On the bright side, Mrs Barnes has raised my wages. I now get £4.98 an hour and so have nearly £20.00 to put in the sadly depleted pickle jar.

Sunday 17th May

Text from Peter @PeterTheTweeter: **Hey guys, I'm on twitter! Follow me!**

Text from me: **No**

Monday 18th May

4.00pm: Art Block

Art exam today. My chosen topic was "The Beauty of Sound" and I have just spent the last six hours painting a scantily clad woman draped over an amp.

Lydia Smart comes up to me, nods at the picture and says, "She's not beautiful, she's a slag."

Lydia is jealous because her picture isn't as good as mine. Also she's flat-chested.

I say, "Yeah, well, that's what you say."

Which as insults go, wasn't great, but thankfully Lydia waltzes off, leaving me to enjoy a metal-stardom daydream in which lots of very unflat-chested women show their appreciation of my artworks and guitar skills!

10.15pm: Inner Sanctum

Yes! I have finally worked out what to say to Michelle next Saturday i.e.: "It's hot in here but that's just you, Michelle, for when I see you it's like the sun comes out in my head. You are the reason for global warming but in a good way. Please let me take you away from all this?" Gesture towards dirty plates, Derek etc.

I'm scared shitless but I'm determined to go through with it. Whatever happens, at least I can say I gave it a go.

Tuesday 19th May

12.30pm: astroturf

Davey's counsellor has told Davey it's tough being a teen.

No shit!

Wednesday 20th May

3.40pm

Went to my last ever Maths lesson today! This has put me in a brilliant mood. I say farewell to Ollie and jog on home where Jasper, the friendly cat from next door, follows me into the hallway.

"Hey dude, you come for a visit?" I say, reaching down to ruffle his fur. "So how's it hangin'? You been chillin' with da ladeez? Swingin' that furry…"

"Er," says Mum, "Michelle from the Duck is in the lounge."

Jesus, what is Michelle doing here? Apart from thinking I'm a complete and utter moron, that is. Still, maybe she didn't hear.

I go in the lounge and find Michelle sat on our sofa.

"Hi," she grins. "How's it hangin'?"

Great!

"Um, fine," I manage, sitting down in the armchair. "So how come you're here? Not that it isn't nice to see you, of course!"

"Mrs Barnes sent me," Michelle explains. "I'm sorry Josh, but she'd rather you didn't come back to work."

"What?" I say. "Why?"

Michelle looks awkward. "It's not that you did a bad job," she says. "It's just, well, that dude Clint…"

"Go on," I say.

"Well, he complained about you hassling his girlfriend."

"What!" I say. "That's rubbish."

"I know," says Michelle. "The guy's a complete nut-job."

"Damn," I say.

"I told Mrs Barnes, you'd never do something like that. I told her you were way too nice, but he comes in most lunch-times you see. He's a good customer."

"Great," I say.

"Well," Michelle says, getting up. "I'm sorry, Josh. For what it's worth, I'll really miss you. Take it easy eh?"

"Oh, right," I say. "Um… Um, it's hot in here…"

"Sorry?" she says.

I take a deep breath and clear my throat. "What I mean to say, Michelle, is that I really like…"

"Cup of tea, dear?" says my mum appearing in the lounge doorway with a pile of clothing in her arms. "I just need to put these dirty pants in the wash for Josh, then I'll get the kettle on."

"Oh, um, no thanks," says Michelle. "I better be off. I start my shift in twenty minutes."

"Uh.. " I say. "Um."

"No problem, love," interrupts my mum. "I'll get the door for you."

My mum leads Michelle through the hall and opens the front door. "Alright, hun. Thanks for popping over."

Kitchen – 3 minutes later

My mother is shaking her head and has her hands on her hips. "How did you manage to get fired from a job washing up?" she exclaims.

"Mum, it was that business with Clint. He's getting back at me for Maddie splitting up with him."

"Well, as much as I am no fan of Clint. I don't see what he has to do with you being fired. The fact is you can either wash up or you can't."

"Mum, of course I can friggin' wash up!"

"Don't swear at me, Josh."

"I said friggin'. Friggin' is not a swear word!"

"Stop that!"

"Mum, I'm going to do some revision," I say. "Oh, and awesome job on the pants thing, by the way. I hope you realise you've completely ruined the one chance I've ever had of getting a decent girlfriend. Or any girlfriend, come to that!"

I storm upstairs, shut the door and punch my pillow over and over until I'm exhausted.

Thursday 21st May – Last day of prison!

2.15pm: Davey's back garden

I'm still gutted about losing my job and Michelle, but it's damn well not gonna stop me celebrating the fact that school is finished. Yep, compulsory education is history! Never again will I have to wear this incredibly unflattering snot-coloured jumper. Never again will I have to listen to Mr Cain drone on about obtuse angles or watch Madam Zizi get animated over reflex verbs.

"Is it safe, do you think?" Davey says. "I mean, we don't want to set the shed alight."

"It's fine," I say. "Chuck 'em on."

Davey slings his PE shorts on the pile of dry branches. "Good bye and good riddance!" he announces.

"See you in hell!" says Ollie, chucking on his T-shirt.

"Your turn, Peter," Davey says.

Peter looks a bit awkward. "Um, I think I might keep mine," he says. "I think the shorts suit me and I can coordinate the T-shirt with quite a few other outfits."

"Peter," I say. "This is the ceremonial burning of the PE kits. We agreed we'd do this."

"You can have my tennis socks?" he offers.

"Fine," I say. "I guess that'll have to do."

Davey lights the pile of clothing and we watch as it kind of... chars. It's not really the effect we were after but it's still, um...

"Very symbolic," coughs Ollie, waving away the fumes.

"Yes," I say.

"What does it actually symbolise though?" says Peter.

"It symbolises freedom from the tyranny of PE teachers and other despots the world over," says Ollie. Which I thought was pretty good, seeing as he's only predicted a C in English.

Then Davey's mum comes out of the conservatory and empties a washing-up bowl of water over the smouldering pile.

"You four are complete nincompoops," she tuts before going back inside.

"Despot," mutters Davey.

After the semi-success of the PE kit sacrifice we decide to head down the park for celebratory drinks, lounging around and chatting up girls... well, lounging around anyway.

Mum has forbidden me from having alcohol, as usual. She says it only leads to trouble. But Mum is still in my bad books from yesterday, so I have no intention of doing what she says. Besides, if I start drinking now, I'll have plenty of time to sober up before going home.

4.30pm: the park (AKA cattle market)

"Wow," I say, viewing the masses of kids in the park.

'Let's mingle," cries Ollie, racing off.

'Charming," says Davey. "Obviously he doesn't want to be seen with saddos like us."

"Well, maybe we *should* mingle," I say. "After all, we're hardly gonna get girls coming up to us voluntarily. Let's split up, try our luck, and meet back here in an hour."

"OK," shrugs Davey and he and Peter head off in the direction of the playground, presumably to chat up some toddlers.

139

I feel a bit alone and am just wondering if the mingling thing was such a good idea when someone pats my shoulder and says, "Hey, you're Josh, aren't you?"

I look round and recognise a girl from school. She's not Michelle but she is quite cute in a chubby, beady-eyed kinda way – a bit like a giant guinea pig.

"That picture you drew for the art exam was awesome," she says.

"Thanks," I say.

"So, d'you wanna sit down and have some cider?"

"Do ferrets have whiskers?" I say.

"Sorry?" she says.

"Yes please," I say.

I sit down next to the girl (whose name escapes me) and try to think of a good conversation topic. She's definitely potential girlfriend material despite the guinea pig similarities.

She smiles at me and I notice her bra strap slip off her shoulder.

"Nice bra," I say. "I expect you get your underwear from NEXT."

"You're kinda weird, aren't you?" she says, giggling. "Have some more cider."

"Thanks," I say, glugging down a load. "So, is it a balcony bra you're wearing?"

"Huh?"

"To offer more, um, support."

The girl shuffles closer. "Would you like to see?"

"Er," I say. "That would be nice."

I finish off the cider and am just about to squint down her top when she jumps back like a startled pigeon.

"What's going on?" says a tall Clint-like person.

"Oh. hi," I say. "Who are you?"

"I'm Amber's brother."

"Who's Amber? Oh… right."

"Who the f*** is this?" the boy asks Amber.

Amber shrugs. "His name's Josh."

"That's me," I say, hiccupping. "Josh the Destroyer!"

Amber's brother gives me a WTF look, then takes his sister's hand. "Come on. What would Dad say if he saw you like this?"

'It was his fault," Amber says. "He pricked my drink."

"Spiked, I think you mean," I say. "I spiked your drink."

"You're in big trouble, kid," says the Clint-like one, letting go of Amber and grabbing me.

"Ow," I squeak. "That's kinda tight. Look, the cider wasn't even mine. It was hers. If anything, she was trying to get me drunk…"

5.05pm

I'm sure there must be a law against shoving someone head first into a rubbish bin, but it's probably not worth pressing charges. Anyway, luckily everyone around here refuses to dispose of their litter properly, so the thing was largely empty.

Largely.

I peel a used condom off my forehead and watch Amber being frog-marched away by her brother…

"Hey, Josh, tough break."

It's Charlene, the girl who was too cool for Scouts. At first, I don't recognise her as she is wearing purple leggings and a bright pink T-shirt with the words "Soul Diva" on.

"Hi," I say.

"Yo," she says, sitting down.

"You look… different," I say. "You still into metal?"

"Nah, I'm into 50 Cent now."

"50 Cent!"

"And N-Dubz."

"N-Dubz!!"

I feel like I've been stabbed in the chest. "But all the concerts you went to," I splutter. "Your Pantera tattoo!"

"Oh, that was just pen."

Pen!! "What about your nose stud?"

"Stuck on with tape. Look, do you really think my parents would let me have a nose stud? I was fourteen!"

I am totally speechless.

"Well," she says, removing an ice-lolly stick from behind my ear and getting up. "Enjoy the rest of the party. And, er, keep metal, dude."

Ha, yes I will keep metal, unlike some people. God, people like that make me sick. They should be killed, cryogenically frozen, brought back to life and then killed again!

5.40pm

"Why are you shredding that stick?" says Peter.

"No reason," I tell him.

"You seem kinda mad."

"I'm not mad, I'm disappointed," I tell him. "People round

here are seriously messed up. I mean, seriously!"

"Fair enough," says Peter. "And, er, talking of messed up, can you help me find Davey? I think he's got pissed and collapsed somewhere."

5.45pm

It's been just over an hour since I saw Davey, so how he could've become pissed already is beyond me. There again, I'm not feeling too great myself.

I look up to see Ollie, wandering towards us, swinging a white carrier bag.

"Booze," he announces happily. "My bro' bought it for us. Where's Davey?"

"I don't know," says Peter. "I think he's lost."

"Oh, he must be around somewhere," I say. "I'll call his mobile."

I locate my phone and manage to call Davey's number. There's some snuffling on the other end and a kind of grunt.

"I think a badger's stolen his mobile," I tell them.

"Nah," says Ollie. "Their paws are too big for the buttons. Ha ha!"

"Davey," I say into the phone. "Where are you?"

There's a bit more snuffling, then Davey's unsteady voice comes on and says, "I'm in a bush."

"He's in a bush," I tell the others.

We look around at the millions of bushes in the park.

"Which one?" says Ollie.

8.30pm: still in the park – one carrier bag of booze and many bushes later

"Ask him to describe the bush in more detail," urges Peter between hiccups.

"What is the bush actually like?" I ask Davey down the phone.

Davey says, "It's green. Can you come soon? I feel a bit sick."

"Let's go up here," slurs Ollie, pointing to an area largely lacking in bushes but full of girls and booze.

Suddenly Peter stops and squints into the distance, "That's not your mum, is it?" he says.

"Huh?" I say. "Nah..."

I stare ahead. About 40 meters away is a short, sinister, Victorian sort of woman, striding our way. In other words, it is my mum and I'm really pissed!

I look around but there is nowhere to hide apart from one very large bush about ten metres away.

"In there," I say. "Quick!"

8.40pm: a bush

"Joshua, I know you're in there," says my mum.

"How does she know that?" whispers Peter.

"Because his trainers are sticking out," replies my mum.

"You idiot," slurs Ollie. "You've given our position away to the ellen, emen..."

"Hi, Mum," I say getting out of the bush and brushing off a few twigs and something that smells worryingly like dog poo. "What brings you to the park on such a glory, hic... burp?"

"You're drunk," says my mum.

"No," I say. "Nooo! I've only had one can of cider."

"And about half a pint of Jack Daniels and several Bacardi Breezers," adds Peter.

"Shut up, Peter," I say.

"Where's Davey?" asks my mum.

"And a bottle of Carlsberg and two Pina Coladas," goes on Peter

"Shut up, Peter!"

"Oh, hi there," says Davey appearing from out of the same bush. "Sorry, were you looking for me? I fell asleep."

9.15 pm: Transept to Forbidding Portal

My mother has just marched every one of my friends back through the centre of the park to their houses. There were still lots of people from school hanging around and they saw all of it. Annoyingly, my friends seemed too drunk to appreciate the horror of what was happening, but I sobered up to feel every mortifying moment.

'I think you'd better go to your room," says my mum.

"OK," I say.

"I'm not cross," she says. "I'm disappointed. Haven't I told you a million times the trouble alcohol causes?"

"Yes, Mum," I say, "and I'm sorry, OK? But why is it such a massive deal? I just don't..."

"One day I'll tell you," says Mum turning away sharply. "Maybe one day soon..."

Friday 22nd May

5.00pm: kitchen

For the after-exam prom we are supposed to go really smart. Mum starts saying that if I used some of my Duck money I could get a nice new shirt but I think she sees from my expression that nothing this side of a mental meltdown will make me spend the Guitar Fund on clothes.

"Mr Pitman was asking after you," she says, passing over a cheese sandwich, which is presumably my tea. "He said you've been having some nice trips down the park."

"Yeah, he's a cool enough dude," I say.

Mum smiles. "I think Minty may be due a walk."

"Hmm, well I think Minty will have to wait a bit," I tell her. "Soon it'll be the summer holidays and I can walk her every day." Steady on Josh, what are you saying? "Or at least a couple of times a week," I add quickly. There's a large hair in my sandwich but it looks like one of Ozzy's so I keep on eating.

"It'd be great if you could give the poor thing a quick run round the block," Mum says in an emotionally blackmailing sort of way. "Just a few minutes. I'm popping round Mr Pitman's about six if you want to come along. He'd love to see you."

"Mum," I say sternly. "I'm about to embark on ten exams. I think I need to concentrate my efforts on those, don't you? Now if you'll excuse me, I'm going to revise."

It's annoying because I was planning on doing some Facebook stalking but the computer is downstairs and Mum'll be hovering, so I go upstairs and begin some Geography. Apparently, crops need between 250 and 500 millimetres of regular rainfall every year. God, agriculture is boring.

I decide to take a quick break and check the old Guitar Fund. Just to see how it's coming along.

£118.32.

This wouldn't be too bad except, thanks to that jerk Clint, I no longer have a proper job. Great! I'll need about 100 more mown lawns and trimmed edges to get anywhere near the Jackson. I feel so annoyed that I send Peter an angry text demanding he start paying me back immediately. I then get the "Extra Special West Country Fudge" Mrs Simpkins gave me for watering her geraniums and devour the whole lot in one go. I notice absently that 100 grams of fudge is 150 percent of my daily saturated fat allowance. I have eaten 500 grams, which means I probably should be dead, but so what. In fact, I wish I was dead. Maybe if I had a stroke or a heart attack, people might realise how mean they've been to me. Mum would be all guilty and… and... Oh God, what am I saying? I mutter a quick apology to Dad and check the alarm clock. It's five to six.

'Hold on, Mum," I call. "I'm coming."

6.10pm: Mr Pitman's

Minty certainly is pleased to see me. She tears around the room like a psychotic fly and snaps affectionately at my ankles.

"Minty loves you," says Mr Pitman. "And dogs are a very good judge of character."

I smile and go fetch Minty's lead from the kitchen.

"Mr Pitman used to be a plumber," says Mum when I get back.

"Really," I say. I'm not sure why Mum has alerted me to this particular bit of information. It's almost like she thinks I should be impressed – impressed by a career unblocking toilets? I think not...

"A very good one, too," she goes on.

"Ah well," says Mr Pitman, waving his hand. "I did OK. 'Course when the arthritis got ahold of my hands I had to retire early."

I make a sympathetic noise.

"You know, Josh, I think it's about time you called Mr Pitman 'Ned'. Seeing as you two are getting on so well," says Mum.

"Um, OK," I say, "Ned it is."

Mum smiles. She has done a lot of smiling today and it's making me nervous.

"Well, er, I'll just go out with Minty then," I say.

"Yes, alright," says Mum. "You're a good lad, Josh."

I have just started walking down the road when I get a text from Peter, probably moaning because I was rude to him.

Peter says, **Dont worry Hav already got £11.35 4u!**

£11.35. Wahey!

Still, it's a start I s'pose.

Minty starts yapping and pulling at her lead, so I say, "Alright, Minty, let's go."

6.30pm: Steve's Music Emporium on way to park

The Jackson has gone!

I press my nose up against the window, rub my eyes and look again, but it's still gone. And recently, too. They haven't even taken the stand out of the window yet. There it sits, mocking me with its black metal emptiness.

I take a deep breath and steady myself against the wall.

Well, it was inevitable. It couldn't wait forever. Some spoilt kid was probably given it for their 3rd birthday or something. I feel my hayfever coming on again but manage to keep it at bay with my sleeve and lots of sniffing. Minty gives me a consoling look and pees next to the Emporium's drainpipe.

"Good girl, Minty," I say. "Sure you don't wanna do anything else?"

Minty barks and I let her drag me to the park where hopefully she will chase and snap at some small children while I annoy the adults by monopolising a swing and wallowing in my misery. :'(

10.15pm Inner Sanctum

I open my notebook and put several thick lines through aim number 4.

Destined to be apart are we
No more will I see your perfection
Wrenched asunder, I mourn your loss
Lke a man who can't get an erection

From the album: *Mournful Loss* by Josh the Destroyer

Saturday 23rd May

6.35pm: kitchen

For most of the day, I continue to mourn the loss of my beautiful, amazing, awesome Jackson but unfortunately life and revision must go on. Or so I'm told. FML.

Sunday 24th May

11.00am: Inner Sanctum

I'm revising trigonometry and Pythagoras' Theorem. Outside, car doors slam as people prepare to go down to the beach for the day. It must be 25 degrees out there. The sun streams into my room and dances on my maths book like a sadistic fairy. Whoever decided to hold GCSEs in the summer ought to be dragged through the streets naked and then have a stake driven through their still-beating heart.

I revise until my mind can take no more of Pythagoras and start on the Past Imperfect Tense. I can forgive the French most things – eating frogs, the Hundred Years' War, Thierry Henry – but I cannot forgive them for inflicting their language on us innocent Brits. They've got five stupid tenses, for God's sake! How French kids learn it is beyond me.

Monday 25th May

Peter texts to say he wishes he could be 100 percent certain he was gay.

I text back to say that the only certain things in life are

death, exams and the constant expansion of the universe, which was quite profound, I thought, and should put Peter's sexuality problems in perspective.

Tuesday 26th May

8.30am: EXAMS!!!!

Oh well, here we go. I touch the photo of Dad in the hall and ask him for luck before heading out the door and into the jaws of hell.

8.55am: corridor, waiting to go into maths exam

Ollie told me that if you write on your skin, it goes into your bloodstream and travels to your brain. Obviously, this is complete and utter rubbish, so why have I written about 600 equations all over my arms, legs and stomach?

10.45am: back out in the corridor after exam

Yes One down, six million to go...

I think I did OK, but I felt a bit weird towards the end, a bit light-headed. Maybe I have blood poisoning from all the biro.

Wednesday 27th May

1.15pm: hall, physics exam

Hannah Harrigan has just run out of the exam room crying. Is there a law against distracting people in exams? There damn well ought to be. I had to start question 3 all over again. I've a good mind to report her to her policeman dad.

Thursday 28th May

Revising.

Friday 29th May

3.30pm: walking home with Peter, Davey and Ollie after English exam

"Who'd you write your essay about?" asks Davey.

"I can't remember," I say.

"I did my little brother," says Peter. "He's so cute. I'm sure the examiner will love to hear how he runs around with his nappy undone and his whizzer hanging out."

Delusional, totally delusional.

"Come on, Josh," says Ollie. "Who'd you write about?"

I lie and say the postman. It's a ridiculous thing to say as I barely know our postman let alone class him as "Someone who inspires happiness in my life", but I can't tell them I wrote about Ozzy. I don't even think ferrets count as people, at least not if you're a stuck-up English examiner. He or she might be a ferret-hater. They may love British wildlife and despise the way escaped ferrets are destroying our native small mammal populations. Oh well, that's English failed then.

Saturday 30th May

10.00am: Inner Sanctum

Revising.

11.00am

Having a short break.

12.00 noon

Still having a short break.

1.00pm

Having a long break.

1.10pm

Working. I have put the washing on, ironed my shirt, done a bit of dusting, matched some socks (more or less), cut my toenails, scrubbed the toilet, weighed myself, weighed Ozzy, weighed my toenails.

Now that that is all done, I can settle down and revise properly.

2.00pm

God, I am so bored with revising. >:[

Sunday 31st May

2.00pm: kitchen

I ask my sister if she will test me on some French and miraculously she agrees.

2.05pm

I have a huge row with my sister about the importance of un and une. My sister says I have to get them right or I will fail my exam miserably.

I say, "Well, I bet you didn't get them right," and she says, "No, and I failed miserably, didn't I? You stupid tw*t."

Monday 1st June

3.15pm: walking home with Ollie

Today was French and Geography. They both went OK but Ollie is worried about his History. He couldn't remember the first thing about the Russian Revolution, so he wrote an essay on sandwiches.

"It's bound to get me a few marks, don't you think?" he says.

"Definitely," I lie.

Tuesday 2nd June

3.00pm: Inner Sanctum

I take a break from revision to practise some guitar. Just because the Jackson has gone doesn't mean I'm gonna give up my dream of becoming a famous metal guitarist.

Anyway, I can now play the pentatonic scale in all five positions in under 20 seconds. I bet even Kirk Hammett would struggle to do that, at least on a pathetic nylon string for 8-year-olds.

Wednesday 3rd June

8.50am: outside hall awaiting English literature exam

Ollie rushes up and says, "You know the book *To Kill A Mockingbird?*"

"Well, yes," I say. "We have been studying it for the last six months."

"Right," says Ollie. "So what actually happens?"

I try to condense the entire plot of *To Kill A Mockingbird* into five minutes. I have never had such a keen audience. About twenty people are hanging on my every word as I go through its various themes, characters, language and style. If the Metal God thing doesn't work out I may have to become an English teacher. FML.

Thursday 4th June – one month till my birthday!

In 30 days time I'll be sixteen. Jesus, I'm getting old!

I hope I don't have a mid-teen crisis like Davey.

Friday 5th June

Text from Peter @PeterTheTweeter: **Why not take a break from revising and follow me on twitter!**

    Text from me: **I'd rather be revising.**

Saturday 6th June

Next week I have exams every day so it's solid revision. See you on the other side...

Six days later, Friday 12th June

3.20pm: walking home from school

Yes, I have made it! I have managed to get through eight exams this week without:

    1: running out the hall screaming

    2: throwing my pens across the room and storming out

    3: getting chucked out due to whispering

    4: getting chucked out due to looking up answers on my mobile

    5: getting chucked out due to consulting notes stuffed into my underwear.

    All these things have happened to one or other of my peers.

Saturday 13th June

2.00pm: park. Only 2 exams to go!

I meet Davey in the park so we can take our minds off exams for a while.

"How's the counselling going?" I ask.

"OK," says Davey. "My counsellor says that my self-esteem is improving all the time. I can even bump into inanimate objects like doors now without apologising to them."

"Well, that's great, Davey!" I say.

"I've also realised that being thin is not the answer," says Davey.

I feel like saying, the answer to what? What is it not the answer to? But it's probably best if we don't get into anything too deep/depressing, so I just ask if his counsellor is hot.

"Not really," says Davey. "She's about sixty and has stubby grey hairs sticking out of her chin."

"Not exactly fantasy material then," I laugh.

"Funny you should say that..." begins Davey.

"Revision, Davey!" I say, jumping up quickly. "We can't put it off any longer!"

Sunday 14th June

4.00pm: Inner Sanctum

Peter texts to tell me not to worry about revising the Common Agricultural Policy as it never comes up.

Thanks, Peter, you could have told me that before I spent the last three hours drilling grants, subsidies and quotas into my poor overworked, undernourished brain.

Tuesday 16th June

9.45am: hall, sitting geography exam

Yes, a question on the Common Agricultural Policy! In your face, Peter!

I'm getting into the swing of exams now. Shame there's only one left.

Thursday 18th June

3.00pm: last exam – RE!!!

I've just written a pretty impressive essay on the moral issues around animal testing. I said that all animal testing should be banned, especially that on ferrets. Instead, people should test on chavs who beat up old ladies. I hope this isn't too offensive. If the examiner is a chav who has beaten up an old lady, I'm screwed.

Anyway, the nightmare is over! Thank God!

At least the exams are.

Life in general goes on, of course.

Friday 19th June

7.30pm: Ollie's house

Tonight there's a sleepover at Ollie's house to celebrate us finishing our exams. His parents have had to go to a funeral up north and won't be back till tomorrow. Generally, Mrs Hargreaves only lets Ollie have a couple of boys round at a time (which is one more than my mum!) but tonight there will be four of us – Ollie, Davey, Peter and me.

I arrive late because Mum has made me drop a bunch of magazines off at Mrs Stokes'. This should only have taken 10 seconds but Mrs Stokes insisted that I come in so that she can see how tall I've grown and quiz me about school. Why are old people so interested in school? I can only think they've forgotten how awful it was.

Anyway, Davey and Peter are already there (at Ollie's, not Mrs Stokes') and have virtually demolished the smoky bacon crisps which is annoying since they are my favourites. We do a bit of Facebook stalking and then decide to watch the three Lord of the Rings films back-to-back. It's quite a challenge, but Ollie has bought loads of pizza, so we feel up to it. We settle down with our food and prepare to be transported to the vales of The Shire.

"Um," says Peter after Bilbo has disappeared dramatically from the festivities and Gandalf has hit his head on Bilbo's ceiling light (very uncool for a wizard). 'Anyone fancy watching something a bit less Hobbity?"

Well, naturally, I'm a big LOTR fan but it does lack a certain something – boobs, to be exact. Not that this should worry Peter.

"Fine by me," I say. "What you got, Ollie?"

"What haven't I got," says Ollie.

He hands over a stack of what look like photo albums but which turn out to be full of DVDs. His parents belong to this club where you order films, copy them and send them back, so Ollie has more films than Netflix.

"As long as it's got action, violence and swearing, I'm good,"

I say after ten minutes or so of flipping through the books. "A bit of female nudity wouldn't go amiss, but I can live without it."

"Can you?" says Ollie.

"For the time being," I say.

How are you on drug use?" says Ollie.

"I'm good with that," I say.

"Mum won't let me watch anything with drugs in," Peter says.

"OK, no drugs. Horror?"

"I'd rather not," says Peter. "I don't like to see suffering faces."

"What? Peter, you are weird! OK, what do you want to watch?"

"How about this?" Peter says, producing a copy of *Up*.

"No!" I say rather too quickly, "Um, me... No wait, my mum and sister went to see that and they said it wasn't very good."

"I heard it was great," says Peter.

"Overrated, they said," I say.

"Well," says Ollie, closing the final album. "That's it. Over 100 films and we can't decide on a single one. Of course, there are...." Ollie grins sheepishly. "No... better not."

"What?" we say.

"Um, well, there are some DVDs on top of my parents' wardrobe. I don't think I'm supposed to know about them though."

"Really?" I say. "What like?"

"Well, the thing is they're right at the back and I can't quite reach..."

"Ollie," I say. "Have you never considered getting a chair?"

Ollie looks embarrassed, which is rare for him. "The thing is,

I worry Dad'll find out."

"The only way that'll happen is if you leave the disc in the player," I say. "And no one would be stupid enough to do that!"

We get a chair from the study and wheel it into Ollie's parents' room. As I am the tallest, I am chosen to risk life and limb on the swivelling thing. It's a stretch but I manage to grab a couple from the dusty depths. They are all copies so they don't have pictures but the titles have been written on in felt tip.

"Yoga for the over forties," I say. "Hmm, that doesn't sound too good... *Painting in oils – unleashing the creative you!*" I look down, "Are you having a laugh, Ollie?"

"Reach further back," he urges.

"OK hold on, what's this? *Confessions of a Stay at Home Mum*. Ah, now we're getting somewhere."

I go up on tiptoes and reach back further.

"*Angie Gets Her Fill. Bonkers in Sweden. Last of the LESBIAN LOVE NEST!*"

I notice Ollie looks a bit awkward. "Wassup?" I say.

"It's just... Well, it seems kinda wrong..."

"OK," I say. "Let's just watch this one. *Big Bertha*. It sounds like more of a laugh than anything."

I put everything back just as I found it and we take *Big Bertha* downstairs.

10.00pm – 2 crazy hours later

Ollie gets up and turns off the TV.

"Jeez!" I say.

'Bloody hell!" says Ollie.

161

"That Bertha made Jordan look like a dude!" says Davey.

"Are you OK, Peter?" I say. "You're not like... traumatised or anything...?"

"No, I am just so happy!" cries Peter, jumping up from the sofa.

"What?" we all say. "Why?"

"Because I'm finally certain I'm 100 percent gay!"

Saturday 20th June

Ollie is grounded – his dad found *Big Bertha* in the DVD player. Luckily, my mum knows nothing about it and I don't think Mr and Mrs Hargreaves are likely to tell her. Jeez, I shall never look at Mr Hargreaves the same again. He seemed such a nice, quiet man, the sort to like pottering around with his tomatoes, waxing his car, that sort of thing. Hard to believe he's a raving sex maniac.

Sunday 21st June

11.00am

It's the prom on Friday. Not that I'll be going, since I have nothing to wear...

11.05am

Brilliant! I have just found the most excellent excuse! I quickly text my friends.

11.10am: kitchen

Ollie has texted back to say I have to go because there will be free booze.

Davey has texted back to say I have to go because there will be free food.

Peter has texted back to say I have to go because he's gonna "come out"!

Guess I'd better find something to wear then.

Monday 22nd June

5.00pm: Inner Sanctum

Mum gets me to try on Dad's old suit for the prom but the jacket is way too big.

"You're not as broad shouldered as your..." she starts to say.

I say, "I know, it's not fair. Why couldn't I have inherited Dad's muscles?"

Mum takes a deep breath, looks about to say something and then dashes out into the hall.

"Er, Mum," I call. "I'm sorry. I didn't mean to upset..."

But she's gone into her room and shut the door.

Tuesday 23rd June

Text from Peter @PeterTheTweeter: **Hurry, the next person to follow me will receive a free bag of smoky bacon crisps!**

Text from me: **Oh, alright then.**

Wednesday 24th June

3.00pm: Mrs Stokes' house

With great reluctance and a sick feeling in my stomach, I try on Mrs Stokes' husband's suit. Mr Stokes has been dead fifteen years and, for all I know, may have died in this suit: it certainly smells that way.

Anyway, thankfully, the sleeves are way too short. Mum nearly yanks them out at the seams trying to make them long enough, but it's no good.

"Blast," she says, looking at my arms accusingly.

"What a shame," says Mrs Stokes. "You look just like my Albert, God rest his soul."

I shake my head as I remove the jacket. "It is a shame," I say. "The suit is great. I would've loved to have worn it."

Mum grabs my arm and ushers me to the door. "Don't push your luck," she growls.

Thursday 25th June

10.00am: Suit-able Attire Fashion Rental Shop with Mum and Nan

"We want a nice cheap suit," Mum explains to the shopkeeper, whose name is Madge.

"Ah," says Madge. "Which of those two criteria is the most important? Nice or cheap?"

"Cheap," says my mum.

I spend the next twenty minutes heaving myself into various

suits, all of which make me look like... yep, a complete knobhead.

"Well, now this one is a little more pricey," says Madge. "But with suits, you know, you get what you pay for."

"Go on, then," moans Mum. "You may as well try it."

I retreat once more into the curtained closet, struggle into the suit and emerge blinking in the light.

"Now that is a nice suit," says my nan, "very Clarke Gable."

Who the hell is Clarke Gable?

"Oh yes," agrees Madge. "Or... Now who is it you remind me of? I know! Bruce Willis. You know, back in his *Moonlighting* days."

Bruce Willis?

But he's bald, isn't he?

And about 50?

Good looking though, I guess. Certainly a babe magnet.

"We'll take it," I say.

7.00pm: Inner Sanctum

Ozzy is sleeping on the suit! Every centimetre of fabric is smothered in his coarse white hairs.

Great. I will now look more like a giant ferret than like Bruce Willis.

Why Ozzy? Why?

8.00pm

Picking hairs off suit.

11.00pm

Still picking hairs off suit. Only about six hundred million billion to go...

Friday 26th June

7.45pm: the prom!

This prom thing is completely over the top. People are going in stretch limos, for God's sake. Needless to say, I have to walk, but at least ther are a few of us, so we're less likely to get yelled at or spat on. I've met up with Ollie, Peter and Davey. Ollie should still be grounded, but his mum spent a "small fortune" on his suit, so he's been allowed to go. Peter shows me the badge he's wearing which says "100% gay and proud". I give him a high five.

We arrive at the "Lofty Oaks Hotel" and I must say it looks very posh.

"4 stars," says Davey, looking up at the sign. "Not bad."

I don't tell Davey that the only hotel I've stayed in was two stars and one of those looked like it was drawn on in marker.

Inside, there's an area for dancing, some tables with food and a small stage with a dodgy looking band. There are girls in long ball gowns everywhere. They look very different to when they were wearing school uniforms. Some look verging on attractive.

"Let's get some food, before it all goes," says Ollie.

This sounds like a plan, so we head over to the tables.

"Oh look, it's the three musky queers," says Lydia.

Great, it's Lydia, Hannah and Becky: my least favourite people.

"Actually," I say, with what I hope is sarcasm. "There's four of us. That maths exam must've been a bit of a stretch, eh Lydia?"

"Did someone say something?" she says, looking round at everyone except me. "Oh no, my mistake."

I decide not to rise to the bait, partly because I have just said something vaguely witty and partly because Davey beats me to it. "You know, for a skinny person you are mighty full of yourself," he says.

Phew! This is cutting stuff from Davey. Clearly the counselling sessions have paid off! Anyway, Lydia looks a bit stunned.

"Well, I may be quite slim," she says grabbing an extra slice of pizza. "But at least I can put on weight. You'll always be ugly."

God, what a cow. "No, he won't," I snap back. "He's getting his nose done as soon as he starts earning, so there!"

"Ssh!" hisses Davey. "Alert the whole damn school, why don't you?"

I must admit things have gone a bit quiet. Quite a few people are looking at Davey, especially his nose.

"Look," I tell him, "there's no shame in cosmetic surgery. Everyone does it. People even get their dicks done."

"Really?" says Peter.

"Yes," I tell him. "They get them lengthened."

"Well, I didn't think anyone would get it shortened!" says Peter, snorting happily.

I grab a few sandwiches and the last remaining Scotch egg and pour myself some Coke – might as well get something out of this sham of an evening.

"So, um, how much does it cost?" asks Peter, hustling closer and causing me to tip my Coke over my sandwich and drop my egg.

"I don't know," I tell him. God, Peter is a pain sometimes. "Where the hell did that egg go?"

"Were you thinking of getting it done?"

"No!" I tell him. "Why would you think that?"

"It's just you seem to know a lot about it."

"Look, I am not an expert on dick extensions! My dick is a perfectly normal 14.6 cm, thank you very much!"

Suddenly the hall has gone quiet again. A few people are giggling into their vol-au-vents. Lydia gives me a disgusted look. Oh God, 14.6 cm... that's probably really small!

"Unextended, that is," I say. "Extended it's... oh I don't know, like a metre..."

OK, there is no hope now. I have exposed myself as a complete tosser with a grotesquely massive dick. Brilliant. I might as well go home and flog myself with a broken bottle.

Except that... Well, I think I see Becky Calbag smile at me. Is it a smile? It looks like one.

Nah, it's probably just a sneer gone wrong.

Saturday 27th June

9.00am: Inner Sanctum

So, I didn't get off with anyone; I didn't get drunk; my Scotch egg was never recovered; everyone thinks I've got a penis deformity and Davey isn't speaking to me. Other than that, the prom thing went pretty well.

One week till my birthday!

Monday 29th June

11.00am: Inner Sanctum

Davey is speaking to me again, but only because he wants to show off his new Xbox guitar game. Lucky for him, I am a very good friend, so I agree to go round and be hideously humiliated.

Also, I am bored out of my brain.

Also, I want to make sure he's getting me a present for my birthday – five days to go :)

Wednesday 1st July

Three days to go!

Thursday 2nd July

Two :)

Friday 3rd July

10.00am

It's my birthday tomorrow. I will be sixteen. I check eagerly under the bed for my leather-bound notebook.

Have I achieved a single one of the things I wanted to achieve before reaching sixteen?

No.

Saturday 4th July - My 16th Birthday!

9.30am: kitchen

It wasn't a sneer gone wrong, it was a smile! I know this because Becky has sent me a card for my birthday. It has a ferret on the front that looks a lot like Ozzy. Inside, she has signed it "Love, Becky X". Not "best wishes" or "from" but "love"! And a kiss too! Talking of kisses, Aunt Sarah has sent me three. Mrs Stokes four. Peter six (bit worrying) and Mum, a whole row, plus she's written "To my wonderful boy". Shame she isn't as nice in real life as she is in her cards.

Anyway, the point is I have a card from a girl – a girl who likes ferrets. It's true that before today I couldn't stand Becky, but that was because she hung out with Lydia. You can't judge a person solely on their friends! Also, I kinda thought she hated my guts, but maybe Mum's right and I am a bit paranoid. From now on I'm gonna try and be a lot more positive about stuff.

I open the remainder of my cards. Nan has given me one with a flashing badge on the front that says "Hooray! You are 12!" Her memory must be playing up again. She's remembered to put twenty quid in though, which is pretty awesome.

Davey has made me a card that is a montage of metal superheroes. He has included a few people who aren't metal, such as Jon Bon Jovi and Freddie Mercury, but this is a common mistake amongst the uninitiated.

Ollie has drawn an excellent and highly pornographic Big Bertha on his. It's very funny but probably not one for the mantelpiece.

"Here you go, bro," says my sister, giving me a smile. "Knock yourself out. It's thirty quid. I've been saving up my tips for bloody ages, so don't go wasting it on metal crap."

I find that my hayfever is playing up and have to quickly wipe my eyes on my sleeve. "Thanks, sis," I say.

"Well," says Mum. "Lots of money for you to spend on our shopping trip."

Ah, yes. Usually I hate shopping but this is because the only things I ever get are shoes and vests and the occasional "tasteful" T-shirt that isn't in any way cool. You may think that there's no such thing as an uncool T-shirt but, believe me, Mum manages to find them and buy them in bulk. I will put up with all this today, however, because I now have fifty quid, and while obviously some must go towards an electric guitar, I'm going to treat myself for once and spend some of it on CDs!

"We'll visit Ned on the way back from town," Mum goes on.

"Ned?" I say.

"Mr Pitman," says Mum.

"What?" I groan. "But it's my birthday. You said you'd take the day off."

"This isn't work, Josh. Ned wants to see you."

"Why?" I say.

"Well, he wants to wish you many happy returns," she says. "You know how he likes to give you a little something on your birthday."

Yeah, little something is right. Last year he gave me a pack of playing cards with breeds of dogs on the back. Everyone knows

I'm a ferret person. The year before, it was a stress ball he'd got free with *The Times*. Been quite useful that, though, to be fair.

3.00pm: town, Debenhams café

Finally, Mum has agreed we can stop for lunch.

"Have whatever you like," she says. "Don't worry about the cost."

This is not quite as generous as it seems given that nothing on the Debenhams menu is exactly Gordon Ramsey, but it's nice to have something other than a sausage roll for a change. I ask for scampi and chips with mushy peas followed by Mississippi mud pie. Mum's eyes look startled for a few seconds but she manages to beat down her phobia of spending and nod her agreement.

Once we're sat down, I toy with the idea of getting out my recently purchased CDs, but one has a lot of blood and dismembered bodies on the front which may upset some of the other diners. I'll have to leave it till we get home. I can't wait to show them to Ollie and the others.

"So can Ollie, Davey and Peter come over this evening?" I ask through a mouthful of peas.

"Well, we're going to see Ned, remember?" says Mum.

"Yes, but surely we won't be there all evening?"

Mum stirs her tea. "You see your friends almost every day," she tells me. "You can invite them over tomorrow."

I'd like to argue and point out that today is my birthday, but it's probably not worth the hassle, especially as Mum has been quite nice to me and I'm trying to be more positive and stuff. Besides, I don't want my scampi to get cold.

6.00pm: Ned's (AKA Mr Pitman's)

Ned's house is like an oven on a high setting, so I offer to take Minty out for a quick run round the block, but Mum says there's plenty of time for that and asks me to sit on the sofa. She gives me a brief, odd-looking smile before sitting down herself.

"Well, happy birthday, son," says Ned.

"Thanks," I say.

"Here you go. Here's a little something from me."

Ned hands over what turns out to be a plastic pack of guitar picks. Wow, this is actually a pretty useful present. There are about six different ones, all different thicknesses and colours. If I'd have been a girl, I'd have probably really liked them. In fact, I do really like them. I line them up in order of ascending thickness. The smallest one is like a sheet of paper (0.3 mm pale blue) the thickest (1.3 mm orange) is a real hard-core pick. You could poke someone's eyes out with this sucker.

"Thanks," I say. "They're really nice."

"Of course they won't be much use for that kids' nylon string you've got, will they?" says Ned.

"Um?" I say.

With a tremendous effort he gets up from his chair, hobbles to the corner of the room and brings out something cocooned in old Christmas paper. It's big and kind of... kind of guitar shaped!

For a second I have what Mum would call a hot flush. My heart starts thudding and my breaths come short and shallow. It can't be the Jackson, can it? Can it? Eagerly, I rip off the paper...

It isn't.

I should have known that the wondrous Jackson would never

173

be mine. However it is a guitar, and although it's not a V-shape, it is an interesting shape – kind of like a dagger. It's green and the make is ProStarUltraSmooth, which sounds a bit like a deluxe brand of condom, but so what! It's an electric guitar and it's mine!

"Thanks!" I say. "Wow, this is amazing!"

"Your mum told me you were saving up for one," says Ned. "I hope you don't mind that it's second-hand?"

"Not at all," I say. "It's awesome."

"Anyway, if you get on OK with it," says Ned. "I'll draw out some of my savings and get you the Jackson your mum says you want. Like the one that was in Steve's Emporium, yes?"

"Huh? Oh no, you don't have to do that," I say, astonished. "Someone else has bought it now and anyway it was really expensive. I mean really…"

"It's the least I can do," says Ned. "For my own flesh and blood…"

"Um, sorry…?" I say. I look at Mum who is leaning forward on the sofa, hands clenched and looking like she's about to throw up.

"I'm sorry, Josh," she says, laying a hand on my knee. "I should've told you this a long time ago."

"Told me what?" I say, edging away.

"Er…"

"Mum?"

My mum clears her throat. "Ned is your, um…"

I grab the guitar and run for the door.

6.50pm: some streets

I walk around the streets for a while gazing in people's windows at their flickering TV screens, but then it starts to rain and I am forced to take cover in the Co-op. I look a bit of a dick wandering around the refrigerators with a green dagger-shaped guitar under my arm, but what's new? I note that frozen minted peas are on offer and that a twin pack of pepperoni pizzas works out 52p cheaper than buying the same pizzas individually. I don't really like pepperoni though; someone told me it was donkey meat. The lady on the till looks a bit peed off and I realise that she's trying to close the shop, so I am forced out in the rain again.

I'm not sure what to do next. I consider going to Davey's but Davey seems loads happier since his counselling and I don't want to put him on a downer. Ollie is a good mate but he's about as understanding as a pork pie. And Peter? Well, Peter is too understanding. I can't cope with his over-the-top sympathy right now.

What I'd really like to do is go to Finland and join a metal band but I have no money, passport or idea which plane to catch.

I am sixteen years old and I haven't a clue who I am.

I thought I knew where I came from
It guided the way like a flame
But now it is raining inside me
And darkness is all that remains

From the album: *Raining Inside Me* by Josh Walker

Sunday 5th July

6.00pm: Inner Sanctum

It's the day after my birthday and the worst day of my life. I am lying on my bed, staring at the ceiling and trying very hard to make sense of things. It wouldn't have been so bad if I'd been the love child of a mad, passionate affair with an international rock star but no, I was the unintended outcome of a fling with an elderly plumber.

My mum has been very quiet. I think she's been trying to stay out of my way for a while, which is fine by me.

There's a knock at the door and my sister appears. Seeing her only adds insult to injury because my sister, you see, is not the offspring of Ned. Suddenly the mystery of why she is so much better looking than me becomes clear – she had a different dad! A cooler, darker, handsomer dad whose photo still sits on the hall cabinet downstairs and probably will do forever unless I can somehow get Ozzy to smash it.

She sits down on the bed and puts her arm round my shoulder.

"You OK?" she says.

Oh yeah, just peachy.

"I'm OK," I say.

"Try not to be too hard on Mum."

Hah! Easy for you to say. Mum has been hard on me since the day I was born!

"Humph," I say.

"If it's any consolation," she says, "Mum only told me the day before your birthday. I don't even think Mr Pitman knew until very recently."

Oh, that's OK then!

"Well, if you wanna come down for tea I've made some beans on toast."

My sister says this with a glint in her eye as if I'm gonna leap up and cry, "Wow, beans on toast. Thanks, sis! Why am I worrying about having lived a lie for the last 16 years when I could be downstairs eating beans on toast?"

"Awesome," I say.

She smiles and turns to open the door.

"But he's so old," I blurt out.

"Mr Pitman? He's not that old. 56, I think Mum said."

"He looks about 70."

"Well, that's the arthritis..."

"Also," I say. "Also. Why did Mum have to wait until now to tell me? Why not when I was like, six or seven or ten or something? Why ruin a perfectly decent birthday!"

"Maybe she thought you would understand more when you were older."

"Wrong!" I say.

"The thing is, Josh," says my sister. "It won't seem like it now, but actually you are lucky. You have a dad who you can spend time with and get to know. I will never be able to do that. When you think about it, it's probably the best birthday present Mum could've given you."

I don't even bother answering that.

"He used to be in a glam rock band, you know," she goes on. "Nimble-fingered Ned, they called him. That guitar he gave you was his."

The door clicks closed softly behind her and I hear her footsteps going down the stairs.

Glam rock! Typical!

I grab the glam rock guitar and check it over. It's not in bad condition. There are a few chips on the body but it gives it a kinda used and abused look which is alright. Also, it's cut away, which makes it easy to reach the higher frets. Talking of which, I count down and find that there are 22...

8.00pm

It has taken me two hours but I have more or less mastered "One" by Metallica. Ozzy seems to like it. He was dancing along in his cage and making lots of dook dook noises. Of course, it'll sound even more awesome when I eventually get an amp and can blast the roof off this shithole.

Anyway, I'm thinking that if I can play this then maybe I really can be a metal guitarist one day. Whatever happens, I still have that.

8.10pm: Transept to Forbidding Portal

At the bottom of the stairs, I do a double take. There are now two pictures on the cabinet: my dad, or rather my sister's dad, and Ned. Ned looks about thirty. He has long curly hair, thick black eyeliner and trousers that seem stuck to his legs!

Mum comes up and looks at the picture with me. "Can I talk to you a moment?" she asks.

I shrug and follow her into the lounge where we sit on opposite chairs. "I owe you an explanation," she says.

"Yep," I say.

Mum proceeds to explain how, sixteen years and nine months ago, Ned came over to fix the washing machine – yes, seriously! Anyway, he got to telling Mum how his wife was cheating on him and didn't love him anymore. How you go from talking about a blocked drain hose to marital problems, I don't know, but they managed it. Well, Mum was sympathetic and being lonely herself, she invited Ned to stay for dinner and Ned was so appreciative that he went out and bought a nice, expensive bottle of wine and one thing lead to...

"Oh my God," I say. "You got wasted! That's why you won't let me drink!"

Mum looks down at her lap and nods.

"And not content with that," I say, "not content with that, you had sex with a married man, got pregnant and lied to everyone about who the real father was!"

"I did tell Nan," she says. "And I would have told Maddie's dad too..."

"Except he went and died!" I blast back.

Mum is dabbing at her eyes now. "It was just the once. Just a silly mistake. By the time I realised I was pregnant, Ned had made it up with his wife and they seemed so happy together...

Well, anyway, I decided to keep it a secret. I think a few people may have suspected, but none of them could prove anything. Not even Shirley Heppinstall, though she tried hard enough."

"Clint's mother?" I say.

Mum blows her nose. "Yes."

"Hmm," I say, remembering what Clint had said in the pub about my family not being all that innocent. "So," I go on. "I'm guessing you decided to come clean to Mr Pitman, I mean Ned, after his wife went off with that Tesco delivery dude."

Mum nods. "I noticed how well you two were getting on and I thought you both deserved to know. Ned was delighted – he'd always wanted children – but I know it's been... harder for you."

I don't say anything.

"Anyway," says Mum, reaching below the chair. "I thought you might like to see this."

Mum pulls out her leather-bound notebook, the same one I found a few months ago in her wardrobe drawer. Now I know what her secret was!

She opens it up near the middle, to the eighties band photos I saw before.

"He was an excellent guitarist," she says, passing me the book. "You must get your musical talent from him."

Mum is quiet while I look at the pictures of Ned and his band. Then, when I pass the book back to her, she says, "I'm so sorry, Josh. Can you forgive me?"

I don't know.

Monday 6th July

7.30am: Inner Sanctum

It's been another sleepless night and I am lying on my bed staring at the ceiling. I seem to be doing a lot of this lately.

I feel gutted that I didn't know Ned when I was growing up and before he got so bad with the arthritis. We could've gone to gigs together. He could've taught me to play AC/DC solos from an early age. We might even have done weird stuff like play football down the park. All this makes me sad and angry. But...

I get that Mum was worried.

I get that we all make mistakes (admittedly hers was pretty massive).

And, most of all, I get that she is really, really sorry and really, really upset, both things that are quite out of character for my mum, especially the being sorry thing.

I also remember something my sister said...

"If you wanna come down for tea I've made beans on toast."

Nope, not that.

"You have a dad who you can spend time with and get to know. When you think about it, it's probably the best birthday present Mum could've given you."

And I guess she's right. I guess it is better late than never. Plus, it's kinda cool, in a slightly ironic way, to have an aging glam rocker as a dad!

I swing my legs off the bed and pull on some clothes.

If I do decide to forgive Mum, then it doesn't mean I'm gonna let her off easily...

7.45 am: kitchen

"How are you feeling this morning, love?" says Mum, pouring me a cup of tea.

"I'm good," I say.

"Did you, er, think anymore about what I asked you yesterday?"

"I did, Mum," I say. "And I've decided that I almost certainly can forgive you. However, things are gonna have to change around here. And I mean seriously change."

"Like what?" says Mum, looking worried.

"Grab a seat," I say.

Tuesday 7th July

2.00pm: Curl Up and Dye

"For f*** sake, sit still," says my sister. "Do you wanna be stabbed in the eye?"

"Let me think," I tell her.

"Don't talk!"

I am wondering if it's a good idea letting my sister pierce my ear. I am her first ever client and she's even more nervous than I am.

"Wait," I say as she lunges at me with the stapler thing. "Are you absolutely sure this is not the gay ear?"

"Jesus! For the nine millionth time. Yes!"

"OK, let's do it."

There's a jolt, a flash of pain and then a feeling of relief that I can still breathe and see through both eyes.

My sister stands back and looks at me critically.

"Wait," she says. "The ear on my left is actually your…"

"Huh?" I say.

"Nothing," says my sister. "Nothing at all. Wow, looks great. Really suits you."

She shows me in a mirror and it does look good. Yay, number 5 is crossed off the list!

Wednesday 8th July

3.45pm: shopping with Ned

I've been getting on really well with Ned, I mean Dad. Today we are shopping in Steve's Music Emporium for an amp!

"A 50-watt one should be fine," says Ned, manoeuvring his wheelchair round to get a better look. "Actually, 50 watts is going to sound pretty loud in your bedroom. It may annoy your mum and sister a bit."

"Cool," I say.

Ned grins and says, "OK, let's start with this one."

I plug the Dagger of Death (as I now affectionately call my guitar) into a Peavey ValveKing, whack up the buttons to ten and launch into "Seek and Destroy" by Metallica.

I manage to play for twenty seconds before Steve runs over and yanks out the plug.

Thursday 9th July

6.10pm: kitchen

Yes! I am now the proud owner of a body piercing and a very loud amp! Plus, Mum has just agreed that I can grow my hair to my shoulders!

"You can always tie it back for interviews and things," says Mum, shaking out the dishcloth. "I've seen a few of these metal people with their hair back and it can look quite neat and respectable if it's properly washed and combed."

"Absolutely," I say. "Um, talking of metal people, Mum, there's something I'd really like to do this Saturday."

"What's that?" says Mum.

Friday 10th July

9.00am – Inner Sanctum

Text from Becky: **Yes I'd love to come. Thanks so much for inviting me XXX**

Oh my God! Tomorrow is my first proper date with a girl!

An actual girl. Of the human variety.

And we aren't just going to Morrison's, the bus station or even the park. We are going to another country!

Saturday 11th July

4.00pm: HMV, Glasgow, Scotland

I feel a bit stupid getting Alexi Laiho to sign the Dagger of Death. Most people have CD covers or autograph books. No one has a guitar, let alone a giant green one, but it's too late now; I can't exactly hide it up my jumper. I look round hopefully at Becky but it's asking too much even of her ample frontage.

Becky and me are standing in a large record store in Glasgow in a long queue at the end of which sit Children of Bodom. Yes, they are here. In the flesh!

I still find it amazing that Mum let me come. She even paid for it! I know she's worried we'll get lost or kidnapped or something but she admits she's got to let me do more stuff. Plus all the worry will be worth it when I give her the "locally made all-butter shortbread" I've bought for her, Ned and Nan!

"Come on, Josh," says Becky.

A small gap has opened in front of me and I rush to fill it, accidentally poking the headstock of my Dagger of Death up the backside of some giant of a metalhead in front. When he turns, he reveals a face part covered in hair. He's like one of those highland cattle you see up here, only not so intelligent looking.

"Sorry mate," I say.

He gives me a "Go f*** yourself" stare, but doesn't look about to gore me to death, so that's a bonus.

A couple of metres in front of me some wise ass hands Janne (killer keyboardist) a bottle of Jack Daniels. Damn, all I have is a half drunk carton of Ribena and some shortbread fingers. Somehow, I doubt they'll be received as eagerly. Why didn't I bring a present? At least I remembered to wear my Bodom T-shirt.

"You're next," says Becky excitedly.

I look up and there's Alexi Laiho staring at me. "Hey, mate," he says. "Want me to sign that?"

I pass over the Dagger of Death.

"Cool guitar," he lies.

"Thanks," I say. "It's my dad's. He was in a rock band. Glam rock, unfortunately, but the genre did spawn quite a few sub-types of more hard core..." Stop rambling, you idiot!

Alexi autographs the guitar and then, just as I'm about to take it back, he starts to play a song on it! And not just any song but "Bed of Razorz", which is one of my all time favourites!

"Nice tone," he says, handing back the Dagger of Death.

I feel a bit shaky and a small boy behind is making things worse by booting me in the ankle to get me to go forward.

"F* * *ing get a move on" someone up the queue yells.

"Yeah, move it, you English tw*t!"

Reluctant but happy, I finally get myself together and manage to leave the shop. Wow, how good was that!

We do a bit more shopping for Becky, then head back to Glasgow railway station, clearing the crowds as we go with the majestic, newly signed Dagger of Death. It's like a fifty-hour journey back on the train, but it's been worth it.

"Can I ask you something?" I say when I carefully get the guitar stored in the overhead rack and collapse in my seat.

"Sure," says Becky.

"What is it about me you like, exactly?"

"Well, you're kind," says Becky.

"Yeah?"

"Like that day in Geography when you opened all the windows to let that bee out."

"Oh yes," I say, remembering. "And everyone said I was a bee-loving tw*t."

Becky nods. "I'm a softie for animals, too," she says. "Once, I bought a very overpriced brownie on Croydon station and gave half of it to a pigeon with only one foot.'

"That sounds like me," I say. "OK, kind to animals. Anything else?"

"And you're good on the guitar."

"Guitar guru, yes."

"But mostly it's because you're weird," she says.

"I'm not weird," I say.

"Yes, you are," says Becky.

"Tell me one way in which I'm weird," I say.

"Well, for a start, most of your Facebook friends are ferrets."

"Actually," I say, "Only half..." but before I can finish the sentence, Becky leans over and gives me a big kiss. Yes! Number 1 on the list is achieved at last. I can't wait to get home and tick it off in my leather-bound notebook.

IS A FERRET RIGHT FOR ME?

Ferrets are almost insanely cute. They are a whole lot cuter than puppies, kittens and even those funny little owls that are about the size of a Big Mac and blink at you while slowly rotating their heads. But is a ferret the right pet for you? The answer is: probably not. Sorry.

The thing is, ferrets (they like to live in pairs if possible) need a lot of time, space, money and attention. You have to buy a whole heap of stuff, like a really big cage, litter trays, food dishes, toys and all sorts of food and treats. You also need to be able to put up with: 1) your stuff getting ruined, 2) your ferret escaping, 3) bad smells! 4) nipping. And nipping can hurt a lot!

But the main downside to ferrets is that they take so much time to look after. Some of this is fun, like playing, which you should do every day. But spending two hours scrubbing out your ferret's cage isn't much fun unless you're a clean freak, and if you're a clean freak you definitely shouldn't be getting a ferret!

Lots of sad ferrets end up abandoned in rescue centres because people thought they were getting an easy, fun pet. Problem is, they were only half right!

ABOUT THE AUTHOR

J. A. Buckle studied Zoology at university, and now works for the national drugs charity DrugScope. As well as writing, she designs websites, helps out at animal welfare charities, plays guitar, and takes her dog for walks. She has two teenage children, and lives in Surrey.

For more exciting books from brilliant
authors, follow the fox!
www.curious-fox.com